RIDING THE WIND

BARBARA GARLAND POLIKOFF

Riding the Wind

Henry Holt and Company

New York

My sincere thanks to Rick Tully, veterinarian, for "vetting" my manuscript, and to Penny Cerchio, owner of Gif and Macho, and Judy Strenke, owner of Malibu, for graciously answering my million and one questions.

Henry Holt and Company, Inc.
Publishers since 1866
115 West 18th Street
New York, New York 10011
Henry Holt is a registered trademark of Henry Holt and Company, Inc.
Copyright © 1995 by Barbara Garland Polikoff
All rights reserved.
Published in Canada by Fitzhenry & Whiteside Ltd.,
195 Allstate Parkway, Markham, Ontario L3R 4T8.
Library of Congress Cataloging-in-Publication Data
Polikoff, Barbara Garland.
Riding the wind / Barbara Garland Polikoff.
p.   cm.
Summary: When an inheritance seems to make it possible for Angie to buy the beautiful Arabian she rides at Smitty's stables, she finds her father and a jealous girl standing in her way.
[1. Horses—Fiction.] I. Title.
PZ7.P75284Ri 1995 [Fic]—dc20   94-36108

ISBN-8050-3492-7
First Edition—1995
Printed in the United States of America
on acid-free paper.∞
10 9 8 7 6 5 4 3 2 1
Permission for the use of the following is gratefully acknowledged:
James Wright, "A Blessing." Reprinted from *The Branch Will Not Break* © 1963 by James Wright, Wesleyan University Press. By permission of the University Press of New England.

For Joan, Daniel, and Deborah Eve,
who have blessed my life

RIDING THE WIND

CHAPTER 1

Angie always loved the moment when she opened the wooden gate of Smitty's Good Luck Ranch and entered the familiar landscape of weathered stables, the red barn crammed with hay bales, and the horses, the beautiful, beautiful horses. Black, chestnut, gray, dappled, they grazed and romped in the large pasture or rested in a companionable cluster under the cottonwoods. Being at Smitty's eased the wrinkles in Angie's moods and made her feel peaceful, the way she felt when she walked in Thatcher Woods, her footfall quiet as that of the deer.

Ardalila III (Lila for short) shared a stable near the pasture with Allison's horse, Shadow, and Smitty's brown mare, Cruiser. As Angie pushed open the creaking door, Lila moved to the front of her stall and nickered a welcome.

"Lila-ba-dila!" Angie crooned, rubbing the horse's silky forehead. "I missed you yesterday!"

Three years ago, when Angie had first seen Lila, the horse was dappled gray, with a dark gray mane and tail. Now she was nearly pure white, her mane and tail a misty gray. She had the fine bones of the Arabian and that wonderful, well-formed head. Angie dreamed that somehow, someway, Lila would be hers. She and Lila, a pair.

"Lila, listen! I have something wonderful to tell you," she said. "This funny old aunt in Seattle just up and died and left Erik and me each twenty-five hundred dollars in her will!"

Lila lowered her head and nudged Angie's hip.

"So, Lila-ba-dila, I have to earn three hundred dollars more. Then I can buy you from Smitty and take you home to live happily ever after!"

Lila nudged against Angie again, this time more insistently.

Angie smiled. "How do you know what I have in there?" She unzipped her ski sweater, took a plastic bag of watermelon rind out of her pocket, and gave Lila a chunk. She had stored the rind, saved from last summer, in the freezer at home.

Lila engulfed the rind with her lips, crunched it down noisily, and waited for another piece.

"No more," Angie said. "We've got work to do."

Taking Lila's red plaid blanket out of the locker, she laid it across the horse's back. It looked neat against Lila's whiteness. The saddle came next and then the bridle.

"Now my turn," she said. First her black riding helmet, pulled down over her hair, then the safety vest her mother insisted she wear ever since she had taken a bad fall.

Angie had wakened that morning to a clear blue sky, but now, leading Lila outdoors to the jumping arena, she saw dark clouds drifting in. She felt chilled but jumping would warm her up fast. Lila's breath steamed in the frigid air.

"Great! We have the whole place to ourselves." Angie opened the gate to the arena and began to walk Lila. "We have to do some serious flatwork to get you warm this morning," she said, pulling up the collar of her sweater to cover her chin.

After they had completed three laps, Angie mounted Lila and they trotted for a while, cantered, and then, just to be safe, Angie walked Lila one more lap.

"Ready?" She dropped the reins and moved the cross rail to the proper notch in the jump standard.

With Angie in the saddle again, Lila trotted around the track one more time.

"Okay, Lila, let's fly," Angie said. Lila, cantering now, headed for the jump.

It was one of those days when Angie and Lila moved as one being, the vibrations passing from Lila's body into Angie's own as she held her knees lightly against Lila's sides. As they approached the jump, Angie fixed her eyes on the far trees. Sensing the moment of uplift, she felt the thrust of Lila's electric leap carrying them over the cross rail, free and light, to land on the ground in one seamless motion.

"Lila-ba-dila, you did great, the best ever!" she exclaimed. They practiced for almost an hour, jumping two feet, then two-and-a-half feet, until they cleared the three-foot rail with the grace of a hawk flying the wind currents.

"Lila!" Angie sang. "Two watermelon chunks today! But first I have to cool you down." She pulled off her helmet, hung it on a post, and began circling the track at a leisurely pace. When she heard the gate open, she looked around. Sage Sommers! She quickened her steps.

"I'll take that horse," Sage said, striding up to Angie and Lila. She was wearing her usual jeans with gaping slits below each knee and a red bandanna tied around her forehead. Thirteen, she was nearly a year older than Angie, but had moved around the country and changed schools so often, she was still in the seventh grade. To Angie's relief, they weren't in the same class.

"We've been jumping and Lila's sweaty," Angie said. "She needs to be cooled down."

Sage's eyebrows lifted. "Horses like Lila can do fifty jumps in a row and not get tired. How many did you do? Three?"

Angie bristled. "You'd better ride Cruiser." She moved past Sage, her heart beginning to race.

Sage's eyes flashed. "You act as if you own that horse!" She turned on her heel and stalked out, the gate swinging wildly behind her.

6

Angie took a long, shaky breath. Cool. She had to stay cool. She slowed her pace and began to hum "Four Strong Winds," to rid herself of the bad energy Sage had pumped into the air.

Sage had been challenging her like this ever since she had moved to the ranch four months ago. Smitty had hired her father to be the ranch farrier. Karl spent most of his time at Smitty's, but he also worked at two other ranches nearby. Nice guy that Smitty was, he told Sage she could ride any of his horses as long as it was free. There were usually plenty available, but ever since Angie had won the last jumping competition riding Lila, Lila was the only horse Sage wanted.

"So Lila, what are we going to do about S.S.?" Angie looked into Lila's dreamy eyes. She found comfort there, but no answer.

CHAPTER 2

*A*ngie led Lila back to the stable and was startled to see Horatio Tuckerman sitting on top of a mountain of hay bales, his head nearly touching a rafter. He was wearing that too-small, manure-colored sweater that Angie hated. When he had first moved to Spring Creek nearly three years ago, all his clothes had hung on him, but since last summer, when he had hit thirteen, he had grown as if he were being squirted out of a tube.

He swung around and looked down at her. "I came to photograph you jumping with Lila."

"I'm sorry you missed us." Angie was careful to keep the pleasure out of her voice. "But what are you doing up there?"

"I needed a dark spot to load the film." He frowned as he looked out of the stable window. "As soon as I got here, these monster clouds hid the sun. It's a conspiracy."

He must have been sweating over that camera, Angie thought. His hair was sticking to his forehead in damp loops. She used to tease him about his curls. Kids usually teased *her* about her red hair. Not Horatio though—he had once blurted out that her hair was pretty. Then he had blushed until *he* was red. She hadn't exactly been cool either.

"Horatio," she said, "I have fantastic news. I'm an heir!"

"You're a what?"

"An heir. And so is Erik. We have this aunt . . . I mean, *had* this aunt who lived in Seattle. Aunt Beattie. She just died and left us a lot of money in her will."

Horatio climbed down one bale, held his camera close to his chest, and jumped to the floor. "She must have liked you a lot."

"Well . . . we didn't see her much. She was a little weird."

"Now you can buy a thousand-acre ranch with a hundred champion Arabians."

Angie laughed. "Well, I almost have enough to buy *one* Arabian!"

"Lila?"

"Lila! Smitty said because it was me, he would sell her for twenty-eight hundred dollars. Aunt Beattie left Erik and me each twenty-five hundred dollars. I've got to earn the rest."

Horatio reached out and stroked Lila's forehead as

Angie walked her into the stall. "Twenty-five hundred dollars is a lot of money!"

"So is three hundred. Smitty's great, though. He's letting me work off some of it by helping Owen teach the little kid's riding class."

"Good luck! It took me forever to earn a hundred dollars to help pay for this camera." He ran his hand over its contours as gently as he had stroked Lila.

"How long was forever?"

"Oh . . . three months. Maybe three and a half."

Angie lifted the saddle off Lila's back and hung it on one of the many hooks fastened to the wall. The stable was the oldest on the ranch, and its wood, weathered to the gray of bird feathers, was permeated with the odor of horses, hay, and manure, an odor that had once bothered Angie but now was like a heady perfume. Horse perfume. She loved it.

"The thing is," she said, "my dad might not let me use my inheritance to buy Lila. He says owning a horse is for rich kids."

"But it's your money!"

"I told him that. It just made him angry." Angie took a currycomb out of her tack box and began working it over Lila's back. "He says buying the horse is just the beginning. It'll cost a lot for upkeep. He's right about that, but I told him I'd put all my birthday money and Christmas money into paying for Lila. And I won't ask for one more thing for the rest of my life. I'll live on bread and water. And I expect to earn some extra money baby-sitting and mucking stalls for Smitty. Owen said he would help Erik and me make our old shed at home into a stable. So there'll be no boarding fee. That makes a big difference."

Lila moved closer to Angie and nudged her face. "Okay, Lila-ba-dila. You're hungry and I talk too much." Angie walked out of the stall to the hay-bale mountain and pulled off a flake. Before she had even dropped it in the stall, Lila tore off a mouthful and began munching.

"What does your mom say about buying Lila?" Horatio asked.

"She used to ride before she was married. She understands how I feel. But my dad . . . sometimes I think the only thing he understands is law. He says the way I've got things set up now is just fine. For mucking Lila's stall and feeding and grooming her three times a week, I get to ride her two afternoons and on Saturday if no customer wants her. So I said, Dad, you didn't want to just visit Mom when you fell in love with her, did you? You wanted to live with her, right? Well, I love Lila, and I want to live with her!"

"That must have gone over big!"

Angie grinned. "Yeah. Like a lead balloon, as my aunt Mimi would say."

"Too bad Aunt Beattie didn't leave you twenty-eight hundred dollars."

"She left me a photograph of herself, too. I feel sort of obligated to hang it up in my room. I don't want to

11

though. It may be mean to say this, but Aunt Beattie was really strange looking. Small, squinty eyes and a long face. Like a horse. . . . Oops!" She reached over and patted Lila's head. "Sorry, Lila. On you it looks good."

She switched to Lila's other side and worked a burr out of her tail. Horatio seemed mesmerized by the way Lila's jaws pulverized the green and brown stalks of hay with the steadiness of a machine. "A horse must have a longer face than any other animal," he said.

"That's so that they can eat high grass without it getting in their eyes."

"You made that up!"

"Nope," Angie said. "God did."

"Really? So why did He give Aunt Beattie such a long face? She didn't eat grass."

Angie giggled. "She *did* eat a lot of salads."

Just then a frigid wind swept through the stable, ruffling the silky hair over Lila's eyes.

"It feels like snow." Angie pulled the stable door closed.

"It figures. Ever since I got my camera, it's been raining or snowing."

Angie filled a rubber pail with grain from the grain barrel, added powdered vitamins and put the mixture beside Lila's half-eaten hay. "I've got to go now, soon-to-be-mine Lila-ba-dila." She kissed Lila above her nose.

"She's really a beautiful horse," Horatio said, running his hand along Lila's back.

Angie was just about to shut the stable door behind them when she heard a yell.

"Leave the door open!"

Sage, leading Cruiser, was coming from the direction of the arena. She strode past them as if they weren't there.

"Is she mad at you?" Horatio asked when they had walked a safe distance from the stable.

Angie shrugged. "She's been like that ever since the jumping competition last month. She's used to winning, I guess."

"And she didn't?"

"No."

"You did?"

Angie nodded. "She told my friend Allison that I won because Lila's a better jumper than Cruiser. So now she's trying to get Lila away from me. That's one of the reasons I've got to earn money fast."

"I've seen her in school," Horatio said. "She's always wearing riding boots."

"And ripped jeans and junky earrings. She moved here four months ago. She lives on the ranch because her father's the farrier—shoes the horses, pares hooves, stuff like that. He never talks."

"Is Sage good at jumping?"

"Too good. She's got great form. She's probably been around horses all her life."

It had begun to snow. Angie pulled a white, furry pair of earmuffs out of her pocket and put them on.

"That's not rabbit fur, is it?" Horatio asked suspiciously.

"Yeah. And I shot the rabbit myself." Angie laughed. "Did you ever hear of an animal called polyester?"

"No. But I have an aunt named Polly Esther."

"Horatio! You're kidding!"

"I'm not. And my uncle's name is Sylvester Esther."

"You made that up."

Horatio grinned. "Uh-uh. God did."

It was getting windier, blowing snow into their eyes as they walked. Snow made things more cheerful, Angie observed. Horatio agreed. Even a beat-up house looked pretty with snow covering the roof, running along the porch railing and settling in a smooth bread-shaped mound on the mailbox.

Angie wished they had a longer way to walk together. She liked walking beside Horatio, the snow making the world a little special. She liked the way snowflakes looked on Horatio's hair. He had great hair, like his mom's. She didn't know what his dad's hair had been like, since he had died before Horatio moved to Spring Creek. Horatio didn't talk about him much, but when he did, she could see how much he had loved him. Angie loved her dad, but he was so different from anyone else in the family. She kept feeling she had to get to know him, like some stranger she had just met. Not her mom. She felt guilty loving her better than her dad, but she supposed that's the way it was for a lot of kids.

Horatio shook the snow out of his hair and pulled on a wool cap. They had come to Angie's street.

"Well, sorry the photography didn't work out," Angie said. "Maybe it'll be sunny next Saturday."

"I hope so. Tell Erik to call me, will you?"

"Sure."

"Well, congratulations on your inheritance. Erik, too. What's he going to do with his?"

"Oh, hoard it, I guess. You know Erik. He's a miser."

"Yeah, you're right. Well, see you." Horatio began to jog, and Angie started walking quickly down Honey Creek Avenue, her boots making sharp imprints on the soft snow. The sky was gray now, but it had a glow, as if it were a theater curtain with lights shining behind it. Now that it was February, the days were getting longer. That always made her feel good. She hated December, when it was dark by four thirty.

Had Horatio come to the stable just to photograph, or could he have wanted to see her too?

His best friend Erik's younger sister? She had to be dreaming!

It didn't matter. Since she had become an heir, she felt good about everything.

Not everything, she corrected herself. She didn't feel good about Sage. Definitely not about Sage.

CHAPTER 3

*Y*ou're going along, doing whatever it is you're doing, and wow, an idea explodes in your mind. And you don't have the slightest clue why it hit you right then. But there it is. Solid as a tennis ball. Yours to bounce around, throw in the air, catch. And to think that what's giving you the idea is that blob in your head, looking like overcooked oatmeal—your brain!

Angie's great idea exploded when she was putting clean silverware in the cabinet drawer. She froze, holding a handful of forks. "Mom! I know how I can help make part of that three hundred dollars I need to buy Lila!"

Her mother looked up from the strawberries she was slicing for pie. Angie had inherited her red-gold hair, but not, as Angie had always mourned, her straight nose and perfect teeth. "Angie," she said, "are you forgetting that your father still hasn't given his okay to buy Lila?"

"I figure the more money I make on my own, the more responsible Dad will think I am."

"Well, what's your great idea?"

"I can hold a garage sale! Allison told me she couldn't believe how much they made, just selling her mom's old dresses and her dad's suits, and furniture they didn't like anymore."

Her mother smiled. "Angie, my old dresses make up my entire wardrobe except for my old pants. And your father, indifferent to clothes as he is, can't afford to part with even one suit. And we like our old furniture."

"But Mom! You said you were going to give a lot of the stuff in our basement to the Children's Aid Thrift Shop, right?"

Her mom nodded. "Right."

Angie beamed. "Well, I'm a child and I need aid right now!"

"Angie, people hold garage sales in spring or summer so they can put things out on their driveways. Not in the middle of winter."

"Oh." Angie's voice dropped. She stood, holding the forks in her hand, her face clouded. Then the light broke through. "We'll just take our cars out of the garage and hold a real garage sale—in the garage! Erik and I can put our bikes and skis in the screen house."

Her mother held up a strawberry, and Angie opened her mouth. She popped the berry in.

"*Ummm*, juicy." Angie reached over and snatched a strawberry slice off the cutting board.

Her mother lifted the knife. "No more!"

"Mom, people will love a winter garage sale. Something different. What about that fur hat of Grandma's that Erik wore last Halloween when he was an arctic explorer?

"Angie, you're incorrigible!"

"Does that mean you're saying yes?" Angie looked closely at her mom and saw a smile playing at the corners of her mouth. "You are saying yes. I can tell!"

That night at dinner Angie brought up the subject of the garage sale. When Erik sat down, late because of band practice, she read aloud the flyer she planned to distribute:

" 'Anxious Angie's Garage and Bake Sale. Chance of a lifetime to go home with that one thing you never thought you'd own. Happy customers are my trademark. Please bring your own shopping bag. This is printed on recycled paper.' "

"Why Anxious Angie?" Erik asked, slathering butter on a whole-wheat roll.

"Because that's what I am. Anxious to make money."

Her father paused, holding a spoon full of soup suspended. He was a tall man, with shaggy, silver gray hair. His penetrating eyes fastened on Angie with

18

what she called his "lawyer's look." "Angie, don't you think that twenty-eight hundred dollars is a great deal of money for a twelve-year-old to spend on herself?"

A flush rose in Angie's cheeks. "But Dad, it's not as if I'm buying expensive clothes or jewelry or hundred-dollar shoes like Trish Sayers! Lila and I have a special feeling for each other."

"No doubt Trish Sayers would claim that she has a special feeling for those hundred-dollar shoes."

"Dad, it's not the same thing!" Angie grabbed a roll and began to spread butter on it, keeping her face turned away from her father.

"*Anxious* Angie's all wrong," Erik said loudly, trying to maneuver the conversation in another direction. "No one's going to come to a garage sale with that stupid name."

"What about Adorable Angie's Garage and Bake Sale?" their mother asked.

"Oh, Mom!"

"Addled Angie?" her dad suggested.

"What does that mean?" Angie asked suspiciously.

"It means mixed-up," Erik said, delighted to know a word that Angie didn't. "Everybody knows that. If I were you, I'd keep it plain. 'Angie's Garage and Bake Sale.'"

"That's because you have no imagination," Angie grumbled. "I like Anxious Angie. I'm going to keep it."

"And is your mother furnishing the baked goods?" her dad asked.

Angie busied herself capturing a carrot in a spoonful of soup. "I haven't checked with her yet."

"Angie knows I don't mind baking a couple of batches of chocolate mocha squares."

"And I can bake some of my killer cookies too," Angie said, looking at her mother gratefully.

Erik gagged. "You'll have to *give* those away."

Angie ignored Erik.

"I'll ask Aunt Mimi to make some of her lemon squares."

"I'll donate those purple suspenders she gave me," Erik volunteered.

"I thought I'd sell the yellow sweater she knitted for me." Angie smiled. "What if Aunt Mimi comes to the sale and sees all the things she gave us?"

Her father helped himself to more soup. "Of course she'll come to the sale. She'll consider it a family obligation."

"I can shrink the sweater to size three by washing it in boiling hot water. She'll never recognize it!"

Her mom shook her head. "Angie, you *are* incorrigible."

"That doesn't mean mixed-up too, does it?"

"No," her dad said. "It means not reformable."

"Oh." Angie thought a minute. "Mom, do you want to reform me?"

"No. Not today, anyway."

"But some days?"

"Definitely."

"Which ones?"

When her mom didn't answer, Angie decided she'd better change the subject.

That night, while Angie was brushing her teeth, she wondered if Horatio knew what incorrigible meant. He had that list of new words his mom had started him on. She'd have to ask him.

As she climbed into bed and pulled the covers up to her chin, she thought about the dinner-table conversation. Sometimes her dad really pushed her buttons!

Addled Angie ... Anxious Angie ... Adorable Angie. No. Not adorable. Definitely not adorable.

Good night, Anxious Angie, she said. And before she could say Lila-ba-dila, she was asleep.

CHAPTER 4

S aturday morning Angie wakened early to a sky turned coral pink by the rising sun. Horatio would be able to photograph today. She didn't admit how glad that made her feel, but she took extra time brushing her hair and put on her best riding breeches.

As she walked to Smitty's, she pocketed her earmuffs and shook out her hair, letting the fresh breeze comb through it. Oh, she was ready for spring, when she would be able to stow away ski sweaters, thermal socks, turtlenecks, and greet the day in the lightness of cotton and sandals.

She saw nothing of the neighborhood; her mind was playing with plans for her garage and bake sale. She had decided to hold it on Saturday, February 27. That would give her enough time to get all the stuff together, send out flyers, and clean the garage.

Sage's father hurried past her as she walked through the ranch gate. He sported long sideburns, a small moustache, and a dusty black cowboy hat that he never took off. He and Sage lived on the edge of the far pasture in a peeling gray bus that Karl had converted into living quarters. It looked like a beached whale caught in the high brown grasses. On one of the windows was a decal of a snake wound around a heart dripping three drops of blood. A sudden, nameless fear had tugged at Angie when she had first seen that snake, its forked tongue darting. It was like the tattoos on the arms of motorcyclists who roared through town in a caravan and stopped at Ginny Mae's Custard Shop.

She shivered and hurried into the stable, dim in contrast with the bright morning. Allison was grooming Shadow, a black stallion her family had bought a year ago. He had been thin then, with a dull coat and a withdrawn air. But with all the care and love Allison lavished on him, he was thriving.

"Sage came and took Lila," Allison said. "I told her you always rode Lila on Saturday mornings, but she looked at me as if I were a worm and took her anyway." Her smile was sympathetic. "Sorry, Angie. I tried."

"What time did she get here?" Angie burst out. She wanted to scream! Or cry.

"Maybe you could ride Cruiser. It's better than hanging around waiting."

"I'm too mad. Cruiser would feel it." Angie shunted off her daypack. "I might as well muck Lila's stall. Fat chance Sage will ever do it."

"Yeah." Allison shook her head. "Sage is bad news."

Angie had dumped the second load of dirty straw when Horatio opened the stable door and walked in, his camera slung around his neck. Whoever had cut his hair had given him his money's worth. He looked scalped.

"The sun's finally out," he said. "Hey, where's Lila?"

Angie tried to sound casual. "Sage took her for a ride."

"But the light's so good now!"

"I thought I'd beat her, but I didn't."

Horatio walked out of the stable and then came back in. He was seething with impatience. "Next time we'll have to get up earlier."

Angie didn't answer. She rested the pitchfork in the corner of the stall, buttoned up her jacket and walked outside.

Horatio followed. He took Angie's cue and said nothing. Angie sat down on an empty barrel, and bit a nail off her little finger.

"Hey, there they are!" Horatio pointed toward the woods as Sage and Lila emerged from the hickories that bordered the pasture. Girl and horse were silhouetted against the blue sky. Angie stood up and walked toward them. "I'll take Lila now," she called as Sage and Lila drew near. "Someone's waiting to photograph her."

Sage brought Lila to a standstill. Her hair fell forward, covering one of her eyes. "Who?"

"Horatio Tuckerman."

Sage frowned. "Who's that?"

"Me," Horatio said, walking up to them.

Sage's cool gaze swept from Angie to Horatio. "What kind of photographs?"

"The good kind," Horatio answered.

"Is *she* going to be in them?" Sage tossed her head in Angie's direction.

Horatio nodded.

"I'm afraid I can't give you Lila," she said. "The poor thing is sweaty. She needs to be cooled down."

"I'll walk her." Anger made Angie's chest and throat burn.

Sage looked down from the regal height of Lila's back.

"Oh, in that case." She dismounted. "I'm always glad to have someone cool down my horse!" The fringe on her leather jacket swung as she walked away.

Horatio waited until she was out of earshot, then pulled up his collar. "Brrr. The temperature's just dropped ten degrees!"

Angie shrugged. She refused to waste another word on Sage. Pressing her cheek against Lila's warm neck she murmured, "Lila-ba-dila, I'm so glad to see you." She walked Lila around the ring twice, then headed for the stall. "Just one more thing, Horatio. I have to clean Lila's feet."

Horatio gave her a puzzled look.

"Horses get junk caught in the grooves in the bottom of their feet," Angie explained. "Have you ever tried to run with a stone in your shoe?"

At the stable Angie took a wooden-handled steel hook from her tack box. She started with Lila's back legs first, stroking her leg to calm her, then lifted her foot and ran the hook through the grooves.

Horatio paced back and forth. "How come you never see Wyatt Earp clean his horse's feet?" he demanded as Angie switched to Lila's other side.

Angie laughed. "You don't see Batman take a bathroom break either. Movies just don't show things like that."

She finished the cleaning, finally, and headed for the arena. Horatio's cheerfulness returned.

"Does Lila like to jump?" he asked.

"Smitty thinks she could be a champion."

"Is that what you're hoping? That Lila's a champion?"

Angie nodded.

"And would you ride her?"

Angie kept her eyes on the two neat triangles of Lila's ears. This was something she hardly ever talked about. "I hope so."

Horatio didn't ask any more questions. Angie liked him for that. He seemed to know when it was time to say nothing. He said nothing better than a lot of adults.

She set the cross rail at two feet while Horatio looked for the best shooting angle. Luckily the sun was at his back.

26

Angie mounted Lila and they trotted around the ring a few times, then switched to a canter. After being on the trail, Lila didn't need much flatwork before jumping. "Lila-ba-dila, we've got to look good. We're having our picture taken." Angie said. "We're ready," she called to Horatio.

Horatio began shooting photographs nonstop. By the time Angie had raised the cross rail to three feet and Lila had jumped over it several times, Horatio had used up two rolls of film.

"That was great," he said as Angie dismounted.

"Thanks to Lila." Angie rubbed Lila's back. In response, Lila swung her head around and rubbed it against Angie's back. The first time Lila had done that, Angie had almost hit the sky. She couldn't believe it! But Smitty had told her that if a horse loves you, it treats you as if you were another horse.

"Were you scared when you first started taking those high jumps?" Horatio asked as they walked to Lila's stable.

Angie shook her head. "Owen says you don't need special talent to jump, just confidence. He starts you with the cross rail lying flat on the ground, and makes sure you feel in control of your horse before he raises it to six inches, and then a foot, and then a foot and a half. So you never do anything you're not ready for. Sometimes he's so careful, it drives me nuts."

"Do you get to gallop with Lila? I mean, full speed, hooves pounding, tail flying?" He grinned. "Like they do in the movies?"

"Yes, but not often enough."

"It must feel awesome."

Angie nodded. "Like riding the wind."

Back at the stable two cats, Honey Bun and Honey Bear, jumped down from the hay bales to greet them. A beautiful golden color, they were sisters and looked exactly alike. Honey Bear, the more affectionate of the two, brushed against Lila's leg.

"Lila loves watching the cats run around the hay bales," Angie said. "They keep her company."

Horatio volunteered to help Angie finish mucking. Lila was tied outside the stall and Angie had given her carrots to munch. The sun streamed in the window, and Honey Bun danced in it, trying to catch the shining dust motes with her paws. Angie liked the easy way she and Horatio worked together, comfortably without talking.

She sighed a small, contented sigh. An hour ago she had felt tight as a drum. Now she was feeling as light and free as one of those bright, dancing dust motes.

CHAPTER 5

Angie found a note taped to the cookie jar when she came home later that day. Her mom knew she wouldn't miss it there, especially when she smelled the freshly baked lemon-drop cookies. Angie also noticed a stack of ashtrays next to the cookie jar. Five of them, probably every ashtray in the house. Puzzled, she read the note:

> *Dear Angie,*
> *Ran out of computer discs so had to take unexpected ride to Prairieville and then stop at the bank. Be back around 4:00. I'm sure you found the lemon drops. Leave some for Erik. Hope you had a good morning with Lila.*
>
> *Love, Mom*

P.S. The ashtrays are for your garage sale. I'm donating them. I quit smoking as of 9:47 this morning.

Angie reread the P.S. once, then twice. She couldn't believe it. She and Erik and her dad had been begging her mom to quit smoking for years. Her mom's compromise was to smoke only when she was writing. That didn't help, because she always had a deadline for her cookbook series and was writing all the time. Angie would drop little reminders that Horatio's father had smoked while he was writing, two packs a day for twenty years, and he died of lung cancer. Even that didn't make a dent.

But yesterday Angie had really blown her cool. At the beginning of the semester she had learned that Harold, the school custodian, had lung cancer. That day she had seen him for the first time since he had returned to work. He had always been a friendly, pear-shaped man. Now he was very thin. With a shock that hit her in the pit of her stomach, Angie realized that he had no eyebrows. He was also wearing a baseball cap, something he never used to do in school. She knew it was to hide the loss of hair from chemotherapy. Not one brown strand poked below the hat. His neck was naked and pink.

She had come home after school and gone up to her mom's study. There was her mom, sitting at the computer, a cigarette in her mouth, smoke circling her shining red hair. That was when she had lost it.

"You know what you're doing?" she had cried.

"You're killing my mom, that's what you're do-ing!"

Breaking into sobs, she had run out of the study, down the stairs. "Do you want to be *bald*, is that what you want?" she yelled from the doorway of her room, then flung herself on her bed and yanked the quilt over her head.

Angie's mom had come into her room, gently re-moved the covers from her face, and held her in her arms, rocking her as if she were a baby.

"Okay," she said. "I hear you, sweetie. I hear you."

That's all she had said.

And now this. The ashtrays and the note. Angie put the note down. So why didn't she feel happy? This is what she had wanted for so long, wasn't it? Instead she couldn't stop herself from crying all over again.

She reached into the cookie jar and ate three lemon-drop cookies. Then she grabbed the ashtrays and brought them into the garage, where she priced four of them at one dollar each, and the blue one shaped like a teardrop at two dollars.

Would her mom really quit smoking? A lot of peo-ple said they'd quit, but they couldn't. But her mom was strong.

Angie breathed a huge sigh. Finally, relief, like healing water, washed out the tightness in her. She went to her room to change out of her riding clothes.

She was doing homework, looking for poems about horses for an English project when her mom came in carrying a loaded shopping bag.

"That's a lot of computer discs," Angie said.

"I needed a few other things, too. I almost bought a jacket to reward myself for giving up smoking."

"You should have, Mom. What was the jacket like?"

"Too many gold buttons."

"You should buy something else then." Angie hesitated. "Mom . . . thanks. For quitting, I mean."

Her mom gave Angie a quick hug. "Angie, I haven't told your father or Erik yet, so, don't say anything. I'll tell them tonight."

At dinner her mom's announcement was greeted with a loud shout and a bear hug from Erik. Her dad kissed her. "That's wonderful news, Beth."

"I want the quitting to be permanent," she said, "so I decided on this strategy. Bernard, I'm going to give you a hundred-dollar bill with a signed note that says if after two months I have not smoked a single cigarette, I get the money back. But if I smoke even one cigarette, I'm obligated to contribute the hundred dollars to the National Rifle Association."

"But Mom, you hate the NRA!" Erik exclaimed, incredulous. "You're always signing petitions against them."

His mom smiled. "That's the point. I had to pick an organization I'd so hate to give one penny to that I'd never smoke again."

"Beth, that's masterful!" their dad said.

"You can't smoke anymore, Mom. I put all your ashtrays up for sale."

"How about a quart of Ginny Mae's chocolate custard to celebrate?" her dad suggested.

"Bernard, you're sweet," her mother said. "But no thank you. While I was writing today, I consumed three mocha yogurts, a half pound of sunflower seeds, and a whole bag of cheddar-cheese popcorn."

"When are you going to give Dad the hundred dollars and the note?" Erik asked.

"This very minute."

They all watched as she pulled the bill out of her wallet and wrote a note. She signed it with a flourish, and Erik and Angie applauded wildly.

"Mom," Erik said. "What made you finally decide to stop smoking?"

"Oh, life works in mysterious ways." Her mom caught Angie's eye and they both smiled.

CHAPTER 6

Angie's spirits were high on Saturday as she walked to the ranch. She and Erik were going to Plummer's Pond that afternoon for the debut as a sled dog of Silver Chief, Horatio's Siberian husky. She was sure her eyes lit up when Horatio had asked her to come. Oh well, she never had been good at acting cool.

She had set the alarm early to insure that she awoke in time to take Lila out on the trail before Sage got to her. But as she opened the stable door, her antennae picked up the fact that Lila wasn't in her stall. Just Cruiser and Shadow in their stalls, and Honey Bear and Honey Bun chasing each other up and down the hay bales.

So this was the way it was going to be—she and

Sage trying to beat each other out and get to Lila first. *Sage*—the name eclipsed the good mood she had been in.

Honey Bear rubbed against Angie's leg, then meowed when Angie ignored her. Angie bent automatically and stroked the cat between the ears. Honey Bun remained aloof, looking down from the top hay bale, kitten of the mountain.

Owen was out in the arena early, giving his five-year-old daughter, Karama, a ride around the ring. He smiled and said good morning. Karama, her small, impish face engulfed by her riding helmet, called proudly, "Hi, Angie. I have new breeches."

Angie's mood lightened at the sight of Owen and his little daughter, whose Swahili name meant "precious gift." Owen was Angie's first and only riding teacher, and she couldn't imagine taking lessons from anyone else. Smitty's right hand man as well as head riding instructor, Owen was always ready to help her when she needed it. He was tall and broad-shouldered, and though he had a severe limp, the result of a bad fall in his horse-racing days, he could walk with surprising speed. He, his wife Carole, and Karama were one of the few African-American families living around Spring Creek.

"You're up with the sun this morning, Angie A," Owen said. There had been two Angies in the beginners' riding class, so Owen had called her Angie A and the other girl Angie B. Now, three years later,

Owen still called her Angie A. She liked that. It made her feel as if she were special to him.

"Did you see Sage and Lila?" Angie asked.

"About fifteen minutes ago."

Angie followed Owen as he walked around the ring with Karama. "Soon Sage won't be able to ride Lila. I'm hoping to buy her. Or did I tell you that already?"

Owen grinned. "Angie A, you tell me that at least once a day."

"Owen, I don't!"

"Daddy," Karama said. "I want to go faster."

Owen quickened his pace. Karama's horse was a perfect animal for a beginning rider. His name was Sir Lancelot, but he was usually called Sir Lunch-a-lot because of his enormous appetite. When he was hungry, he'd nibble on anything, including scarves and hair.

"Sage got the idea that Lila's a better jumper than Cruiser, and that that's why I won the competition. So now the only horse she wants to ride is Lila." Angie shrugged. "But beside that, I get the feeling she likes to give me a hard time."

"Sage needs friends," Owen said. "Human friends, not horses."

"She sure doesn't act like it!"

"She may be afraid to, Angie A."

Was Owen asking her to be a friend to Sage? He probably was. He was so softhearted. Enough of Sage!

"Owen, I'll walk with Karama if you have things to do."

Karama wasn't sure she wanted to give her daddy up, but she liked Angie and decided to let Owen get some work done in the tack shack.

Angie's anger slowly ebbed away as she walked Karama and Sir Lunch-a-lot. Karama was happy just to be riding. Life is so simple when you're five years old, Angie thought. For a moment she felt a yearning for long-gone days when she was as young as Karama. She couldn't remember a thing that had interrupted the honey-smooth flow of her life when she was five. Not a thing.

When Angie and Erik arrived at Horatio's house, Horatio's mom, Evie, announced that she was going with them. "I wouldn't miss it!" she exclaimed, pulling a tasseled wool hat over her black hair. Angie thought she looked much younger in a down jacket and boots than she did in her white dentist's clothes. She really liked Evie.

O.P., Horatio's grandfather, accompanied them to the door. So did O.P.'s dog, Sky. O.P. wasn't able to walk down the rocky hill to the pond. "I've lost the salt of youth," he said. "Sky and I will have to rely on you to tell us what happens."

Angie guessed the words "salt of youth," came from Shakespeare. O.P. (which stood for Old Professor) was always quoting Shakespeare.

A light snow was falling. Perfect weather for sledding, they all agreed. They made a cheerful parade on the road to Plummer's Pond: Horatio, his camera slung around his neck, pulling the sled; Erik carrying the ropes and harnesses; Evie walking with Silver Chief on a leash; and Angie holding a bag of dog treats.

Horatio ran down the hill to the pond, calling back that the ice under the snow was as smooth as glass. It was a cloudy day but windless, and snow blanketed the high, wheat-colored grass surrounding the pond. Black trees were etched against the gray sky and red berries still clung to bushes at the head of the pond, the only spattering of bright color.

Angie and Evie watched as Erik and Horatio struggled to coax Silver Chief into the harness. The husky seemed alternately bored and impatient with the procedure.

"Silver Chief, Dog of the North!" Evie exclaimed as the harness was finally in place, fitted snugly around Silver Chief's chest and back.

Horatio hooked the sled rope to the rear metal loop of the harness. "Angie, you go first," he said. "You're the lightest."

Angie wasn't that eager to be first, but she sat down on the sled and held on to its sides. Silver Chief turned and looked back at her. He seemed puzzled by what was going on.

"Ready?" Horatio asked, excitement flushing his face.

"Ready," Angie answered.

Horatio began running. "Silver Chief," he shouted, "Let's go!"

Silver Chief's ears flattened, his tail straightened, and he sprang forward. The sled skimmed across the ice behind him. Angie screeched, half in fear, half in ecstasy. Erik ran behind the sled, shouting wildly. Evie waved her hat and cheered.

As the sled raced over the ice, Angie leaned forward. Trees and bushes whizzed by. Her hood blew off and the cold air made her scalp tingle. She fixed her eyes on Silver Chief's outstretched tail, a white plume flying in front of her. Oh, it was wonderful!

At the edge of the pond the ice petered out and Silver Chief crashed into the stiff grass, the stalled sled restraining him. Angie rolled off, laughing, as Horatio and Erik ran up to her. She was covered with snow. It was in her mouth as she hugged Silver Chief.

"Silver Chief!" Horatio yelled. "You did it! It's in his genes," he said to Evie as she ran up to them. "He knew just what to do!"

Evie hugged Angie. "You were great." She turned to Horatio. "Congratulations!"

Horatio grinned. "Hey, Mom. How about you going next?"

"Thanks for the honor, but I'm happy to be the cheering section."

"Are you sure?"

Evie nodded. "Very sure."

Horatio sat down on the sled and Angie and Erik started Silver Chief off, running beside him, Erik hollering "Mush!" as if Silver Chief knew what "mush" meant! Horatio yelled joyfully as Silver Chief pulled the sled across the frozen pond.

Erik took his turn, and then they each had second rides. Horatio managed to shoot a whole roll of film.

On her next run, Angie took a belly-flop position on the sled. With her face closer to the ice she felt she was going even faster. But when the ice ended and Silver Chief ran into the bordering grass, the sled slammed into a half-sunken log and jolted to a sudden stop, catapulting Angie onto the ice. She landed with her arm under her body, her hand twisted. She screamed and rolled over, holding her arm against her. Her wrist throbbed as if bands of fire encircled it.

"Angie, are you all right?"

Horatio and Erik hovered over her, their anxious faces peering down. Evie ran up and bent to wipe the snow off her face.

"My wrist," she said, barely managing the words. "I think I broke it." Her mouth was dry. She felt nauseous.

"Rest a minute," Evie said. "When you think you're ready to walk, we'll get you to the emergency room."

Angie sucked back a sob. "I'm ready now," she said. She wasn't going to cry!

Erik helped her back up the hill, and Horatio ran ahead with Silver Chief, leaving the sled behind to pick up later. He wanted to get to the house to call Angie's parents, as Evie had suggested.

No more laughter. Just the sound of feet trudging

through the snow. How quickly the world can change, Angie thought, holding her throbbing wrist close to her body.

Beth and Bernard weren't home. Evie drove Angie to the hospital, Erik and Horatio in the backseat. She spoke with the emergency-room doctor who examined Angie's wrist and ordered an X ray. The bad news was that the wrist was broken; the good news was that it was a hairline fracture. The doctor put the wrist in a cast and gave Angie some pills to ease the pain.

Exhausted, Angie leaned against the backseat of the car as they drove out of the hospital parking lot. How could one spot hurt so much?

"Who's going to muck Lila's stall now?" she asked miserably.

"Smitty will get someone to do it," Erik said. "Maybe I can get to the ranch sometimes and help out."

"I'll try to get there, too," Horatio said.

Angie tried to keep her voice from quivering. "This is going to slow up getting ready for the garage sale."

"Everything looks dark now," Evie said. "Tomorrow you'll figure out how to manage."

Angie laid her head back on the seat. It felt good having everyone around her. She took a deep breath and let it out slowly. She didn't dare move her arm. "Silver Chief did great, didn't he?" she said.

Horatio nodded. "It's in his genes."

The car hit a pothole, joggling Angie's arm. She gasped and squeezed the tears back.

"Are you all right?" Horatio asked.

He looked at her with such concern that in spite of her pain she felt a puff of pleasure blow up—a balloon, rising.

Evie was right. She'd manage.

CHAPTER 7

I can't believe you do this every day," Erik said as he tossed a pitchforkful of urine-drenched straw from the floor of Lila's stall into a wheelbarrow.

"You do it if you don't want your horse to get thrush. It's an awful foot disease. Really smelly." Angie put the currycomb back in her tack box. She had been grooming Lila for the last hour. The horse's coat gleamed. At least there was something she could do with one hand.

Erik heaved a sigh. "I'm glad I like drums. You don't have to clean up after them."

Erik dumped the last load of straw into the wheelbarrow. "That's it! Hey, can I get a drink somewhere?"

"Why don't you bring in some clean straw from

the pile outside the stable and I'll get you a can of soda."

Angie blinked in the bright sun as she walked out of the stable.

"Hi, Angie," Allison called, riding by on Shadow. "How's your wrist?"

"Better, I guess. Thanks."

Trish Sayers, one of the older girls who boarded a horse at the stable, was walking out of the tack shack as Angie hunted in her pocket for some coins. Even Trish asked her how her wrist was, and Trish wasn't famous for being interested in anybody but herself. The ranch was like a small town. Everybody knew everybody else's business. Sometimes Angie liked that; other times she didn't. Trish had very expensive riding equipment. Angie suspected that she spent more time buying riding clothes than riding.

She inserted the coins into the machine and a can of root beer clattered down the shoot. She couldn't resist opening it and taking a drink.

Back at the stable she heard the sound of voices. She paused, listening. Sage! If Angie were a cat, she would have hissed and arched her back.

Erik was leaning on the rake handle talking while Sage put the saddle on Lila. She was actually smiling. It figured. Erik was a guy. I'll bet she doesn't smile when she sees me, Angie thought.

Angie charged in and handed Erik the root beer. "I'm going to do some lunging with Lila," she said to Sage. "I just went to get Erik a drink."

Sage took the bridle off a hook and proceeded to put it on Lila. "Lila doesn't need lunging," she said. She spoke slowly, as if addressing someone who had trouble understanding English. "She needs to get out on the trail."

"I'm going to buy Lila. So you might as well get used to another horse."

Sage tossed her hair back from her eyes. "Smitty's selling her?"

"Right."

"How much is he hitting you for?"

"That's between Smitty and me."

"Well, Lila's not your horse yet!" Sage grabbed the reins, colliding with Angie as she led Lila out of the stable. "Smitty could change his mind," she shouted over her shoulder. "He's been known to do that."

"How do you know what Smitty's been known to do!" Angie shouted back. She wheeled around. "Erik," she said in a fierce whisper, "I hate her! I really hate her!"

Erik let out a low whistle. "You two were ready to scratch each other's eyes out."

"I bet you think she's really cool!"

Erik grinned. "Not bad. What's she ever done to you?"

"Why do you think she's so cool? She's really short. Practically a midget."

"You still haven't told me what she's done."

"She's the one who's always stealing Lila."

"Why is she baiting you like that?"

Angie lifted her chin. "Because I'm tall and beautiful and one of the best jumpers at the ranch."

"Yeah," Erik said. "That's probably it."

There was no point in being at the ranch now, so Angie walked home with Erik. She said nothing the whole way home. Erik kept himself company by whistling.

"Mom," Angie called as she ran up the long stairway to her mother's study. Her mom was sitting in her easy chair, editing a manuscript. A bag of cheddar popcorn was on the floor at her feet.

"Mom! Dad absolutely has to let me use my aunt Beattie money to buy Lila!"

Her mom looked up from her editing. "Angie! You look upset."

"That cowpie Sage! She grabbed Lila just when I was going to lunge with her. With this dumb wrist, I can't ride, so I couldn't stop her."

Angie's mom rose from her chair and laid a manuscript on the desk. "Angie, maybe you should try to be a little more understanding. Sage hasn't had a lot of the advantages you've had."

"Does that give her the right to give me a hard time?"

"Today was really bad, then?"

"The worst! Ask Erik. . . . No, don't ask Erik. He thought she was cool. Boys! All they care about is what a girl looks like!"

Her mom smoothed Angie's hair back from her forehead. "When your father sees how hard you're working to help pay for Lila, perhaps he'll come around."

Angie picked the popcorn bag up from the floor and coaxed out a few remaining kernels. "Mom, Smitty can't just decide that he doesn't want to sell Lila to me, can he?"

"Here's the man to answer that legal question," her mom said as her father walked into the study.

"My checkup went well," he said, dropping a kiss on her mom's lips. "I guess the two of you will have to put up with me for a while. The doctor couldn't find anything seriously wrong."

"Did he find anything that *wasn't* serious?" her mom asked.

"My blood pressure is up slightly and I've gained too much weight."

"Dad, if Lila were mine and lived here, I could teach you to ride and the pounds would drop off!"

"You're sure of that?"

"Dad, it's an emergency! Sage keeps stealing Lila and I can't do anything about it!"

"Angie, not now." Her father left the room.

Angie exploded. "Mom, Dad's . . . so . . . stubborn!"

Beth picked up the bag of cheddar-cheese popcorn, found no popcorn in it, and threw it in the wastebasket. She took a fresh bag out of the bottom drawer of her filing cabinet and tore it open. "I'll talk to him again, Angie. But you know your father. He has to come around in his own time."

"That won't be until the twenty-first century!"

Angie watched as her mother put a handful of popcorn in her mouth. "Mom, isn't it a little too close to dinner to be eating all that popcorn?"

Her mom closed the bag and put it back in the drawer. "You're right. Which reminds me—I have a casserole to put in the oven."

The mail was stacked on the kitchen counter. Angie stopped to leaf through it. Every once in a while there would be a catalog that she liked to look at.

Nothing today.

Her room was so cold that she pulled off her shoes and crawled under the quilt. That was the big advantage of not making her bed. She didn't worry about messing it up. She lay on her back and stared at the black silhouette of a hawk she had taped to her window to discourage birds from flying into it.

"Angie."

It was her mom. Time to set the table for dinner. She wished she could eat in her room, but eating dinner together was a sacred family ritual. Mostly she liked it. Not tonight.

"Angie! Horatio's on the phone."

She jumped out of bed. "Coming," she yelled, and dashed for the stairs.

CHAPTER 8

I asked my mom if she'd bake some of·her apricot slices for your sale and she said she would, Horatio told Angie. "They're the best."

Angie felt a twinge of disappointment that Horatio had called to talk about the sale. But then, what had she wanted him to call about? She felt the heat rise in her cheeks. "That's great."

"I got the photographs back that I took of you and Lila."

"Oh, are they good?"

"Some were off by just a split second. But there's one I like."

"I can't wait to see it."

"I saw your Anxious Angie flyer in Ginny Mae's the other day. And one is pasted on the hardware-store window."

"I have nightmares that no one will come. It's a good thing the sale's this Saturday."

"Did you collect enough stuff?"

"Pretty much. A few things turn up every day. My uncle just dropped off his old golf set. I'm really getting antsy, though."

Horatio laughed. "Antsy Angie's Garage and Bake Sale."

"That's me," Angie said. "Antsy Angie."

Angie woke at seven Saturday morning and tried to lie quietly in bed and relax. No use. She got up, threw on some clothes, and went downstairs to the kitchen. Her mom was there, eating oatmeal and reading.

"The gods are smiling on you," her mom said. "It's a clear day. The prediction is for snow tomorrow, which doesn't make me happy since your father and I are flying to New Orleans for a lawyers' convention."

Angie tucked her denim shirt into her jeans, then zipped the fly. She had trouble pulling the zipper the last two inches. "Mom, either these jeans have shrunk or I'm getting fat."

"Any shrinking those jeans did happened a long time ago. You're obviously getting fat."

"You really think so?" Angie turned her profile toward her mother and ran her hand over her stomach. "Do I bulge?"

Her mother studied her. "Terribly. I'd stay away from sweets for at least another hour."

"I'm getting fat because I don't get any exercise riding." Angie paused. "Mom, do you think people will come today, or am I going to sit in the garage with those teacups and Barbie dolls and no one but Aunt Mimi and Uncle Harold will show up?"

"Mimi and Harold can't come. They're visiting Harold's father in Indiana."

Angie let out a monumental sigh. "Well, I suppose I should be glad. Aunt Mimi might have recognized that yellow sweater even though I overdid the shrinking. All it will fit now is a guinea pig."

Her mom looked at her closely. "You've got rings under your eyes, Angie. I don't think you'll rest until Lila's yours."

"I'm going out to the garage, Mom. Maybe there'll be some early customers."

Horatio and O.P. were the first to arrive. Horatio was toting a large tray of apricot slices, which Angie directed him to put on the bakery table with her mom's mocha squares and Aunt Mimi's lemon squares. Erik's comment about her killer cookies had cooled her confidence, and she'd decided not to make them. She'd never let Erik know he had scored, though.

"Those apricot slices smell so good!" she said.

"They're more than good," O.P. said. "They are superb!"

"I'll buy some of those," her father said as he walked into the garage. He was wearing old brown cotton pants that ballooned in the knees and a white sweatshirt with a faded picture of the Teton Mountains. "Good morning, Professor. How are you, Horatio?"

"Dad, look at the picture Horatio took of me jumping with Lila." She held up a photograph that Horatio, acting very matter-of-fact, had handed her.

"You're a real professional, Horatio."

Horatio colored with embarrassment. "Thanks."

"Horatio said I could keep it."

"Be ready to relinquish it, Angie. Your mother will want to hang it in the family gallery."

Their next-door neighbor Mrs. Tattle poked her head into the garage. "I thought I might be too early."

Her dad said a hasty good-bye and ducked out through the kitchen door. She knew he didn't want to get stuck talking to Mrs. Tattle. He hated small talk and was terrible at it. Every July 4, when the neighborhood had a party, he hid out in her mom's study.

"You want those mocha squares, Mrs. Tattle? They're over on the bakery table. Mom baked two dozen."

"And what is this divine goody?" Mrs. Tattle asked, sniffing the apricot slices.

"Those are Horatio's mom's famous-the-world-over apricot slices."

"Millard will adore those. He's wild for apricot."

"One cannot desire too much of a good thing," O.P observed. He was going through a carton of old books Harold and Mimi had donated.

When Mrs. Tattle left, Angie put the cash for the pastries in a metal box. "Well, my first sale."

"Add four dollars more to that, Angie," O.P. laid two books and four single dollar bills on the table where Angie sat with her cash box. "Good luck, Angie. Horatio, call me when you want to be picked up."

Just then Erik stumbled into the garage, looking half asleep. He must have planned to wear that shirt with those pants, Angie thought. Such an ugly combination wouldn't just happen.

"Here's a customer," Horatio whispered, pointing to an elderly woman who had just walked in.

"She may buy a cup and saucer. Maybe two cups and saucers," Angie said.

But the woman left without buying anything. Then a mother, father, and their three children came in. The little girl went straight to Angie's old Barbie dolls. She ended up with two of them. Her father bought Bernard's old golf clubs. A good sale. Angie's spirits were rising.

By eleven o'clock there were at least a half-dozen people milling around the garage. Allison was right, Angie thought. It was amazing what people would pay good money for. One very tall woman bought all of Mrs. Tattle's terrible jewelry. Another woman bought the shrunken yellow sweater and a waffle iron donated by Allison's grandmother.

At noon the garage emptied out and Beth served a vegetable pizza. Angie, Horatio, and Erik crowded around the table.

"I've only made fifty-five dollars," Angie said. "I see no one's bought my ashtrays."

"Don't worry, Mom," Erik assured her. "I'll buy them and throw them in the trash can."

"Hey, here come some cup-and-saucer ladies," Angie said.

She was right. Two women who owned a small collectibles shop called Lost Treasures in Prairieville bought all four sets, as well as a tall, pink bedroom lamp.

"This guy's going to buy the fur hat," Erik said as a stocky, bearded man walked in. He circled the garage slowly and actually did buy the fur hat. It turned out that he was the costume designer for the university theater.

Erik and Horatio left to play soccer and returned around four. The last customer had just wandered out. Angie decided to call it a day. The items that remained wouldn't bring in much anyhow.

Horatio and Erik hovered over her as she counted the receipts. One hundred thirty-five dollars.

"I had hoped to at least get a hundred and fifty," she said disconsolately.

"Do you know how many leaves I had to rake to make a hundred dollars?" Horatio asked. "Tons!"

Erik and Horatio decided to go sledding with Silver Chief while Angie packed up the unsold items to give to the Children's Aid Thrift Shop. She was so restless that evening that she called Allison and told her about the sale in excruciating detail.

"If not for Sage, I wouldn't be hyper about buying Lila so soon," she confided. "But I feel like she's some evil spirit waiting to swoop down and take Lila away."

"Don't worry so much," Allison said. "Lila's practically yours now."

Later, in the shower with the water going full blast, Angie crooned, "Lila-ba-dila, when, oh when, will you be mine?"

CHAPTER 9

*A*ngie's parents had to drive to Milwaukee the next morning to catch a plane to New Orleans. Angie knew her mom had never been to New Orleans and was eager to hear good jazz and eat Creole food. They were just going to be gone two nights and had arranged for Aunt Mimi to stay at the house, though Angie and Erik insisted that they would be fine by themselves.

"And Angie," her mother said. "Remember your wrist. I think you overdid it at the sale yesterday."

By the time their parents drove away, Angie and Erik were glad to see them leave. They both agreed that parents could be exhausting sometimes.

"I'm going to the stable," Angie said.

"It's so crummy out. What is it, raining or snowing?"

"It's hard to tell. Maybe both."

"I suppose I should go and muck Lila's stall for you."

"Horatio said he'd do it this afternoon."

Erik breathed a sigh of relief. "Good."

Angie shivered when she stepped outside. Rain was changing to sleet. It was nasty. Kind of the way I feel, she thought.

She tried to pull herself out of her bad mood by thinking about which name she would engrave on Lila's bridle when Lila was finally hers. Some horse owners engraved the names of their horses and then their own names underneath. Should she put the full name, Ardalila, or just Lila? "Ardalila. Owned by Angie Mordell." Or should she use her full name, Angela Mordell?

She was so caught up in her musings that she was surprised to suddenly find herself opening the gate to the ranch. The place seemed deserted. Owen was in the roofed arena working with a small boy on Gentle Sue, a chestnut mare Owen often used for beginning students. Angie poked her head in the arena, waved to Owen, and then headed for Lila's stable.

Lila was not in her stall! Tears of frustration welled up in Angie's eyes. She brushed them away furiously. She had figured that the bad weather would have stopped Sage from taking Lila on the trail. Not Sage!

The wind forced Angie to put on her earmuffs as she hurried back to the arena. The temperature was dropping. There was a skin of ice on all the puddles.

Owen was leading Gentle Sue back to her stable. Angie fell in step beside him.

"That's a mean wind kicking up," Owen said.

"Yeah, and Sage took Lila out! I feel like telling Smitty. He should know the crazy things she does."

"Sage is a good rider, but she has to learn respect," Owen said.

"For what?" Angie asked, just for the satisfaction of hearing him criticize Sage.

"Respect for everything . . . the weather, the horse . . . herself."

Angie and Owen were heading for the tack shack when they saw Sage break out of the woods and race toward them. Her face sent Angie's heart into her stomach.

"Owen!" Sage shouted. "Lila fell on the ice!"

"Is she down?" Owen began to run.

Angie bolted ahead of him. Horror stories about horses that injured a leg and had to be put down flashed through her mind. New ice gave way under her pounding boots and the wind hammered her face. By the time she reached Lila, the horse had pulled herself up and was standing, head lowered, mouth gaping, eyes unfocused.

"Oh, Lila!" she cried.

Owen ran up to them and began talking gently. "Lila, how are you, sweet lady? Now just let me see if I can feel anything on this leg. Lila . . ." As Owen spoke, he ran his hand along Lila's lower front leg.

When he reached below the knee, she grunted with pain.

Angie pressed close. "Owen, is she all right?"

"She's hurt her leg." He stood up. Sage was hanging back. She looked terrible.

"Sage, tell Smitty to get the vet out here. Quick!"

"I'll go," Angie said. "She's done enough!"

Fighting cramps in her stomach, the frigid wind turning her tears to ice, Angie ran what seemed like a hundred miles to Smitty's office.

CHAPTER 10

S mitty had a box stall available for Lila, although he didn't seem all that happy about putting her in it. But Dr. Rago made it clear that Lila had to have stall rest for as long as two months, and needed the twelve-by-twelve space. Unlike the regular stalls, the box stall had enough room for Angie to pull a chair into it and sit, keeping vigil, talking to Lila to soothe her and let her know she wasn't alone.

Angie was leaning back in the chair, resting her head against the wall, her eyes closed in half sleep, when Horatio's voice startled her.

"Angie! Owen told me you were here. What happened?"

Angie stared at him, trying to bring herself back into the present. Her head felt clogged. She had trouble sorting out words. "Oh ... Lila's hurt. She fell. On the ice."

"Is it bad?"

Angie stood up so quickly she knocked the chair down. "Sage," she said. "It's practically an ice storm and Sage takes Lila out on the trail!" The memory of Lila, hurt and in shock, overwhelmed her. She took a long, shuddering breath. She spoke as if trying to recall a distant event. "Lila slipped and hurt her leg. Dr. Rago thinks she has something called a green-stick fracture, but he has to look at the X ray to be sure."

"Which leg?" Horatio asked.

"The right front one. The fracture's on the inside splint bone. It's behind the bone that's between the knee and the ankle." She laid her cheek against Lila's silky mane. "Lila-ba-dila, does your leg hurt very much?"

Horatio's face was sober. The last time he had seen Lila she had been jumping the cross rail, a picture of power and grace. Now she stood, her bandaged leg slightly off the ground, her head drooping, her powerful body tense as if all the muscles were wired too tightly.

"What does it mean to have a green-stick fracture?" he asked.

"It's not a complete fracture. If it had been ... well, we're lucky it's not, that's all."

"It sounds like Lila had a pretty close call."

"Anyhow ... you know if you try to break a branch that's not dead, but still alive and green, it splits into

61

a lot of strands and won't break? Well, that's what a green-stick fracture is like. Lila will probably need at least two months stall rest, and her leg has to be kept in a thick, very tight bandage. Almost like a cast."

"Wow," Horatio breathed. "She'll go bananas."

"What about me?"

"You're going to take care of her that whole time?"

Angie nodded. "Smitty doesn't have anyone free to do it. Lila needs her bandage changed every other day or she might get pressure sores." She hesitated, worrying over a thought, and then continued. "Erik thinks I shouldn't try to buy Lila now. I should wait and see if she'll be okay and if she'll take a rider again." She turned and thrust her hand into the warmth of Lila's mane. "But . . . Lila's my horse whether I get to buy her or not. You know what I mean?"

Horatio nodded.

Angie caressed Lila's forehead. "She's hurting a lot. Dr. Rago doesn't like to give pain pills because if the pain is numbed she might move around and that would be bad for her leg."

Horatio moved closer to Lila and gently rubbed her forehead. "After the stall rest, then what?"

"I'll have to ease her into walking. The first week, ten minutes two times a day, then the next week, ten minutes four times a day, the next week twenty minutes four times a day. Until Dr. Rago says she's back to normal."

"And then will you be able to ride her?"

Angie averted her face. She felt the sudden threat of tears. "If everything goes all right . . . we'll have to see."

"I'm really sorry, Angie."

She nodded but didn't look at him.

"Lila, you're going to get better, I know it," Horatio said.

"I decided not to leave Lila alone tonight, Horatio. I'm going to sleep here. Erik thinks I'm a little crazy, but he's going to stay with me. He'll bring our sleeping bags and we'll sleep outside the stall."

"Is that okay with Smitty?"

"We're not asking. Erik will wait until after dark so no one sees him."

"You look really tired."

Angie rubbed her eyes. She knew she looked terrible. She hadn't eaten since breakfast, although Erik had brought her two peanut butter and jelly sandwiches from home.

"Do your mom and dad know what you're doing?"

"They're in New Orleans at a lawyers' convention. My aunt Mimi is supposed to come to our house and sleep over. We'll have to figure out something to tell her. She'd freak out if she knew we were going to sleep in a stable."

Horatio lowered his head. He was thinking. Angie recognized the posture. It was if he had a feedbag on and was silently chewing thoughts. "I've got an idea," he said after a moment. "I'll stay here with you guys. Then Erik can tell your aunt that you won't be home tonight because you'll be staying with Horatio. Which will be true."

Angie felt unreal, and yet Horatio, standing beside her, was very real. "Do you think your Mom will let you sleep here overnight?"

"If I tell her about Lila, she'll go along. I'm pretty sure."

"Horatio, I'm used to it, but this place is smelly and the floor is hard."

"I'll do fine. I want to stay with you guys."

Angie's pulse quickened. "Well . . . if we tell Aunt Mimi that we're going to be with you, it would be the truth, wouldn't it? I just hope she doesn't ask too many questions."

"Kids are always sleeping over at each other's houses."

"And she knows Erik and you are best friends. And your mom is her dentist. So she'll feel it's okay to . . ." Angie managed a smile. ". . . stay with you."

"Is Erik home now?"

"He had a science report to finish."

"I'll get my sleeping bag and then come back here with him. I'll bring a ground cloth."

Angie nodded. "Good idea."

"Do you need anything?"

"Yeah! Hunt up that airbrain Sage and tell her to stay away from Lila and me. Far away!"

"She must be feeling pretty awful about what happened."

Angie shrugged. "What do I care what she's feeling?"

Horatio stroked Lila's forehead. "Good-bye, Lila-ba-dila." And then he was gone.

Angie reached into her backpack and pulled out a peanut butter and jelly sandwich. "Lila-ba-dila," she said. "We're not going to leave you alone tonight. No way."

"Angie A," Owen said. "You better go home now. Lila will be all right. I'll look in on her early in the morning."

"Owen, she's hurting really bad. I can tell. Her muscles are all tense."

Owen's face was sympathetic. "She's hurting. But you'll be hurting too, unless you go home and get some food and sleep."

Angie sighed. "Owen, it would be easier if Lila would complain, be mad and crabby and make a lot of noise. But horses are so quiet when they're sick. It makes me crazy to think she's just standing there, hurting and miserable."

"I know, Angie A." Owen ran his hand lightly along Lila's back. "You're going to be all right, sweet lady. All right."

"She is, isn't she, Owen?"

"If love can make a horse well, she's as good as new right now. Can I give you a ride home?"

"I'm not going yet, Owen."

"Lila's lucky to have you, Angie A."

He was almost out the door when he turned back to look at her. "Sage is hurting too. She's locked herself in the bus and won't come out. She wouldn't talk to me."

Angie's voice was stony. "I just don't want her near Lila."

Owen looked like he was going to say something else, but then gave up on it. He waved to Angie and walked out into the cold evening air.

CHAPTER 11

*H*oratio swept the area outside Lila's stall. "That's as clean as I'm going to get it," he said. It was dark in the stable except for a small circle of light cast by a flashlight propped against the wall. Angie was afraid to put on the overhead light in case someone at the ranch had stayed late and would see it.

Erik stretched out the ground cloth. "I suppose you want to be in the middle," he said as Angie unrolled her sleeping bag. "It's the warmest spot."

Horatio put his bag on the other side of Angie's.

"Girls stay warmer than boys," Angie said. "We've got more blubber."

"Then I'll put my bag in the middle," Erik said.

"It's good the way it is," Angie responded quickly. Why don't you keep your big mouth shut? she fumed to herself. Always something to say about everything.

"I'm crawling in now." Erik pulled off his shoes and disappeared into the bag, head and all. "Feels good," he said, his voice muffled by down.

Horatio wriggled into his bag and rested his head on his rolled-up jacket.

"Good night, lovely Lila." Angie picked up the flashlight, pulled off her boots, and crawled into her bag, leaving the flashlight near her head where she could reach it. She wanted to have it near in case Lila needed her during the night.

She lay on her back, conscious of her breath entering and leaving her body. In the darkness every sound and feeling was exaggerated. Sandwiched in between Horatio and Erik, she could hear the faint clockwork of their breathing. She could hear her own breath, regular as a metronome. All living things breathe, each in its own way, she thought. . . . Deer and fox, wolves and eagles, the wheeling hawk, the butterfly, and the beautiful, beautiful horses. She was overcome by a sudden feeling of connection with all creatures resting from the day, as she was on this cold February night.

She closed her eyes and lay very still. When a feeling like this overwhelmed her, a cosmic feeling, she called it, she would feel dizzy, as if she were spinning in space, unanchored as a dandelion seed. She would have to ground herself by holding her pillow close and focusing her eyes on something ordinary, like her reading lamp or the shoes she had left on the floor.

"My sleeping bag smells of the mountains," Horatio said. "I wish we were in the Rockies and had a campfire and were lying out under a sky packed with stars."

"I can smell the marshmallows toasting over the fire," Angie murmured.

"You smell marshmallows?" Erik poked his head out of his bag. "That's not what I smell!"

"Erik, you have as much imagination as a slug!"

"Angie, do you really think Dad's going to let you use your twenty-five hundred dollars to pay for a horse that has an injured leg?"

Angie thrust out her good arm and jabbed him in the stomach. "I don't want to talk about that now!"

"Yeah, Erik. You're about as sensitive as a toilet seat," Horatio said.

Angie giggled.

"That's not original. I got it from Holden Caulfield."

"Who's he?" Angie asked.

"A character in a book. *Catcher in the Rye.*"

Erik disappeared into the depths of his bag. "Stop yaking, will you? I want to go to sleep."

Angie knew she wouldn't sleep for a while. She rolled over, bumped into Horatio, and quickly rolled back. It didn't take long before Erik was breathing regularly in his cocoon. Angie wished she could sleep as easily as he.

She didn't know how much time had passed when she heard Horatio's whisper.

"Are you up?"

"Um-hum. I keep thinking about things."

"Yeah. Me too."

"What kinds of things are you thinking about?"

Silence. And then Horatio answered. "My father."

"Oh."

"Being in this sleeping bag makes me think of our camping trips in the mountains."

"Did your mom go too?"

"Most of the time . . ." Horatio's voice faded. Angie could hear him shifting positions. She didn't know what to say. She waited.

"I used to believe that when you died, you were dead and that was it."

"You don't believe that anymore?"

The pale moonlight coming through the window outlined Horatio's profile. To Angie it looked older than his full face. She was very close to him, even though they were separated by two thick down bags. They were almost alone, with Erik sleeping like a baby. She let out her breath slowly.

"This thing happened to me. . . ." Horatio's voice was soft. "I had gone for a walk in the woods. I went alone because I wanted to take some pictures. I got so caught up in light and shutter speeds that I lost the trail. And it was beginning to get dark. Fast. Like it does in the woods. So I began to panic. Really bad. Nothing looked familiar. And then, just as I was really losing it, I heard my dad's voice telling me to be calm and to begin walking in a circle that got bigger and bigger and after a while I would hit the trail.

So that's what I did. And it worked. When I finally got to the road, I didn't hear him anymore . . . as if he knew that I was all right, and it was okay to leave."

Angie wanted to reach over and take Horatio's hand. Let him know she understood. But she lay very still. "It must make your father's dying easier if you can hear him talk to you."

"Yeah . . . even though I was scared while I was walking those circles in the woods, a part of me felt good. Really good. You know what I mean?"

"Well . . . I'm not sure. No one I've loved has ever died."

"It's awful."

"Yeah. I get scared when I think about it."

"But it's awful for you now too, with Lila getting hurt."

"Yeah," Angie breathed. "I keep getting these terrible pictures in my head. . . . I see Lila trying to walk and she can't . . . but she tries . . . and crumples to the ground." Her voice broke, and the tears she had been holding back flooded her eyes. She buried her face in the sleeping bag and tried to stop sobbing, but she couldn't.

She felt Horatio's hand on hers. It burned into her.

"Lila's going to be fine with you taking care of her," he said. "I know she will."

She held on to his hand and was finally able to stop crying. Her head ached. But she didn't dare move. If she did, Horatio might take his hand away. She didn't

want him to do that. The warmth from their inter-
laced fingers coursed through her whole body.

After a few minutes, Horatio withdrew his hand.
"I'm starving," he said, sitting bolt upright.

"Wait a minute." Angie crawled out of her bag and
made her way carefully to her backpack. She fumbled
around and found the peanut butter and jelly sandwich she hadn't eaten. She checked on Lila, then
crawled back into her bag and handed the sandwich
to Horatio.

"Thanks!" He tore the sandwich into ragged halves
and handed her one.

"It tastes good," she said. "I could hardly get it
down before."

They sat, eating, not talking.

"Horatio, thanks for sleeping here tonight," Angie
said as they settled back into their bags, the last
crumb of sandwich devoured.

"Yeah . . . well, thanks for listening to me."

"I liked listening."

Finally she was able to fall asleep.

CHAPTER 12

Angie was nervous. When her parents returned from New Orleans, they had received a call from Smitty asking if he could meet with the three of them at his office the following evening. There was something he wanted to talk about.

They had arrived at the ranch early. Her dad had been asking her questions during the entire ride. Having a lawyer for a father was a pain sometimes. As Angie escorted him and her mother to the stable, Bernard kept up the cross-examination.

"I understand, Angie, that you have to change Lila's bandage every other day. How are you going to manage that with your wrist in a cast?"

"I've been practicing. I can do it."

"Do I hear music?" her mom asked as Angie pushed open the stable door.

"That's Owen's old radio playing in the stall. It keeps Lila company."

Lila raised her head when she heard Angie's voice.

"How are you doing, Lila-ba-dila?" Angie stroked Lila's forehead.

"If you put on a program with voices, Lila might have the comfort of thinking people were around," her mother suggested.

"There's nothing but a lot of stupid soap operas and talk shows during the day. I don't want Lila's mind zapped with junk."

Her mom smiled. "Oh, I see."

Angie opened the stall so that her parents could see Lila's bandaged leg. "What does this sound like, Dad?" She bent down and thumped the bandage with two fingers.

"I don't know that it sounds like anything."

Angie thumped the bandage again. "This bandage is made by winding three layers of cotton quilting around the leg where the metacarpal bones are, and then enclosing that in some more layers of Ace bandage. If I've done it right, it's almost like a cast. When I thump it, it should sound like a ripe watermelon."

"Did you learn all that from Dr. Rago?" her dad asked.

Angie nodded. "Lila has a high fracture near the knee, so it has to be wrapped this way. The bandage is named the Robert Jones wrap after the man who invented it. Dr. Rago calls it a Bobby Jones."

Angie's dad looked at his watch. "It's time to go to Smitty's office," he said.

It was clear that he was anxious to leave the stable. They were silent as they walked to the small frame building housing the ranch office. A carved black stallion mounted above the door was still strung with tiny Christmas lights. Smitty liked the lights and sometimes didn't remove them until summer. Smitty was at his desk talking on the phone. He was the thinnest person Angie had ever seen. The girls at the stable joked that anyone who hugged him would get a paper cut.

Smitty nodded in greeting and motioned them to sit down. His office was neat and welcoming. Framed photographs of champion horses hung on every wall, and a tall cactus in a clay pot stood in a corner, doing service as a rack for two of Smitty's many cowboy hats.

When he finished his call, Smitty stood up, and shook hands with Angie's parents. To Angie herself, he tipped his hat.

"Well," he said, sitting down. His Adam's apple rode just above his shirt collar. Angie found herself staring at it.

"I'll get right to what's on my mind. Lila's been hurt bad and needs a lot of care. Not just physical care, but psychological care. I'm shorthanded here as it is. I don't have anyone with the hours to give to Lila. Frankly, she's a burden to me now. She has to be checked regularly by the vet, and when the leg is healed someone will have to hand-walk her daily for at least a month. She'll probably recover, but she may not. Now, Angie knows this, so I'm not saying things out of court. If Lila does carry a rider again, she may not be up to jumping. That puts a special strain on a horse." He paused. "You folks want any coffee?"

"No, thank you," her mom said.

Angie's dad shook his head. "I've had my quota for the day."

"Well, Angie's sitting on nails, I can see that." Smitty smiled, and his deepset eyes almost disappeared under his eyebrows. "I have an offer. I said that I would sell Lila to you folks for $2,800. If Angie still wants Lila, with all it takes in money and time to nurse her back to health, I'll sell her to you for eight hundred. If you don't take her, I'll find another buyer."

Angie couldn't believe what she was hearing. Eight hundred dollars! She looked at her father, trying to read his face. She couldn't. She never could.

"Smitty, is it possible that Lila may not have a complete recovery?" Angie's mom asked.

Smitty nodded. "There can be complications. A bone splinter, broken off because of the fracture, or damage to the ligament under the fracture. Nasty stuff like that."

Angie's heart was beating so fast she could hardly breathe. Why didn't her mom stop asking questions?

"Angie tells me you have land enough to keep a horse at your place." Smitty refilled his coffee cup from a large thermos.

"We do," her mother responded.

"Lots of space!" Angie burst out.

"Angie," her dad said, fixing his eyes on her with his lawyer's look. She braced herself for what was to come.

"Do you realize that while you're nursing Lila, you'll have no time to ride any other horse?"

Angie nodded.

"It's going to be hard on you, Angie." her mother said. "Harder than you may think."

Angie turned from her parents' serious faces. She felt like busting out of that office. She knew what she wanted to do about Lila. Why were they trying to mix her up?

She swallowed hard. "Lila's my horse," she said. "I'm going to take care of her whether I can buy her or not."

Her parents looked at each other. There was a long silence. Then her father turned to Smitty. "Angie seems committed to Lila," he said. "We accept your offer."

Angie jumped up, tripping on her mom's foot as she flung her arms around her father. She couldn't speak. Blinking back tears, she hugged her mom.

Her mom kissed her. "Good luck to you and Lila."

Angie was surprised to see that her mom had tears in her eyes too.

Smitty rose from his chair and took one of the hats off the cactus. "You can board Lila here the first month," he said, setting the hat down over his forehead. "I don't think she should be moved. I'll just charge you the price of a regular stall."

"I'll use all the Aunt Beattie money that's left to pay for whatever Lila needs," Angie said. "And all my allowance money and birthday money and Christmas money, just like I promised." She turned to Smitty. "Owen's going to help Erik and me make a stall in our empty storage shed. It'll work out great."

"Smitty, you're being very kind to Angie," her mom said. "We're grateful."

"That horse is Angie's," Smitty said. "Those two belong together."

Angie risked getting a paper cut and hugged him. Embarrassed, Smitty did his best to hug her back.

CHAPTER 13

Angie's dad dropped the bombshell at dinner the next night. Smitty had called his office that morning with a legal question involving a man who worked at the ranch.

"Do you know Karl Sommers, Angie?" her father asked.

"He's Sage's father."

Her dad buttered his roll before going on. "Yesterday the police came to Smitty's office looking for a check forger. They had some information that made them suspect Karl. Smitty speculates that Karl saw the police, hid out until dark, and then made a getaway in Smitty's station wagon. It was gone this morning and so was Karl."

"A car thief!" Angie repeated, staring at her father.

"And a check forger!" Erik added.

"Did he take Sage with him?" their mother asked.

"Apparently he took off while Sage was sleeping. He left her a note, a photograph of her mother, and a hundred-dollar bill. She's locked herself in the bus and won't come out. Owen's the only one she finally agreed to talk to.

"Wow," Erik said. "Sounds like a bad TV show."

Angie's mom passed her a platter of scalloped potatoes. Angie took one spoonful and passed the platter on. She loved scalloped potatoes, but at that moment they didn't look good to her.

"Well," her mom said, sitting back in her chair. "What a sad turn of events for Sage."

"Dad, do you know how big the checks were that this guy Karl forged?" Erik asked.

Their father ignored Erik's question. He took the platter of potatoes from Angie. "I understand Owen tried to convince Sage to come to his house for a while, but she refuses to budge."

"She can't just stay in that bus," Angie said.

"I'm going to fill a cooler with food. Sage has to eat." Her mom turned to her. "Do you want to bring it to her or should I?"

"You better bring it," Angie said.

"I'll drive you to the stable in the morning and you can show me where the bus is."

"It has to be early, like at seven. I have to change Lila's bandage."

"Seven will do it."

That night Erik came into Angie's room. She was trying to read a new book the librarian had recommended. She was having trouble concentrating. Her mind flipped back and forth like a windshield wiper. Sage . . . Karl . . . Sage.

Erik flopped on her bed. "I wonder if Sage knew her father was forging checks."

Angie put a pencil in the book to keep her place. She was sitting on her bed, propped up against her pillows. She wasn't in the mood to kibitz with Erik. "I don't know and I don't care. I don't like to think about it, either."

"That bus you showed me they lived in—geez, what's it like inside?"

"Erik, I don't want to talk about it anymore. Okay?"

Erik stood up. "I wonder if that hundred dollar bill Karl left for Sage is a counterfeit."

"Erik!"

Erik walked out of the room, then stuck his head back in and grinned. "Pleasant dreams."

Angie scooped up a dirty sock and threw it at him. "Get lost!"

Was it Angie's imagination or did the bus look more battered than usual? The blinds were down. No light showed through the windows. She had never realized until now that objects had a sense of

81

life about them. This bus had no life. It was a corpse.

"Mom," Angie said, "You're sure you want to do this?"

"You take care of Lila. Don't worry about me." Her mom started walking along the edge of the pasture, carrying the red and white cooler that she had filled with sandwiches, fruit, cookies, and drinks. Angie watched her for a second, then turned and ran all the way to Lila's stable. She didn't know why she was nervous. She just was. Everything seemed fuzzy this morning, as if she were living in a slightly out-of-focus photograph.

Her mother appeared just as Angie was finishing the bandage around Lila's leg. Angie was relieved to see her.

"It took some talking," she said. "But Sage finally opened the door and took the cooler. She looked exhausted. She thanked me though. Then slammed the door."

"She's got to come out of there." Angie felt sorry for Sage and at the same time resented that the circumstances of Sage's life forced her to feel sorry for her. It was easier to be plain mad at her. Fuzzy. Everything fuzzy.

"How does Lila's leg look?" her mom asked.

"The swelling hasn't gone down much. And the hurt area is so hot. I'm worried."

"Perhaps you should check with the vet."

"And she's hardly eaten anything."

"That's probably normal, Angie. I noticed you went pretty light on your favorite scalloped potatoes last night."

"Well, maybe I'll splurge and buy a bag of Mrs. Pasture's Horse Cookies. Lila usually just gets those for her birthday and on Valentine's Day."

"I'm sure we can bake some if you found out what the ingredients are." Her mother bent down and thumped two fingers against the fresh bandage. "It does sound like a ripe watermelon. You did a good job."

"I've been massaging the leg above the fracture. The bandage cuts circulation off a little."

"You're learning a lot about horses, aren't you?"

Angie nodded. "And I'm going to learn more. I want to be an equine vet like Dr. Rago. There aren't many, which is good. I won't have so much competition."

Her mom smiled. "I see you've thought it through."

Angie nodded. "A hundred times." She hesitated. "Mom, if Sage's father gets caught and is put in jail, what will happen to her if she doesn't have relatives to live with?"

"She'll probably become a ward of the state and be placed in a foster home."

"With people she doesn't know?"

"Most likely."

Angie let her breath out slowly. "It was good you brought her food."

"I hope she eats it. Do you want a ride to school?"

"Sure. Just let me turn on the radio for Lila. She likes what you and Dad call schmaltzy music."

"Schmaltzy music?" Beth put her face close to Lila and began singing. When Angie had been a little girl, Beth had always sung her to sleep when she wasn't feeling well.

"Home, home on the range,
where the deer and the antelope play . . ."

Lila lifted her head, and her ears twitched forward.

"Mom, she loves it. Look at her!"

When she finished the song, Lila nuzzled her shoulder.

Angie giggled. "She's asking you to sing it again."

Her mom stroked Lila's forehead. "Some other time, Lila. I've got a book to write."

Angie liked when her mother wore her hair in a ponytail. Today she had tied it with a narrow purple ribbon. "That ribbon looks nice in your hair, Mom," she said as they walked to the car.

"Thanks."

"Are you still eating all those bags of cheddar-cheese popcorn?"

"I've been cutting back."

"How are you doing? Quitting smoking, I mean."

"Come up to my study. You'll see where I've chewed off a corner of my desk and kicked holes in all the wastebaskets."

"Mom," Angie began worriedly.

Her mother smiled. "I won't start smoking again, Angie. Don't worry."

Angie sighed. "I wish I could give you twenty-five dollars to keep, and if I bit one nail I'd have to give the money to the Wisconsin Coon and Fox Hunters Club."

"Why don't you try it?"

"You just threw your cigarettes away. I can't do that with my fingers! They're with me, all ten of them, all the time!"

Her mom laughed. "I see your point."

"I'm like a horse. When they're bored or nervous, they chew their stalls. I chew my nails."

Her mother put her arm around Angie. "All this hasn't been easy on you, and I think you're handling it with amazing good spirits."

Angie blushed. "Well . . . I love Lila."

They had been riding along Sweetwater Road for ten minutes when Angie finally managed to get out the words she had been rehearsing since her mom and dad had returned from New Orleans.

"Mom, you know the day that Lila fell? Well, that night I didn't want to leave her alone in a strange stall. She was in pain and so upset, so I slept in the stable and Erik and Horatio kept me

85

company. We laid our sleeping bags on the floor. Erik and I knew Aunt Mimi would freak out if we told her what we were going to do, so instead we just told her we were staying with Horatio. Which we were, really."

Beth took a moment to absorb what Angie had said. "Aunt Mimi would have freaked out, you're right about that. You were being purposefully deceptive, though. You understand that."

"Yeah, but there was no other way. I knew you would have let me stay with Lila if you had been home."

"It must have been a long night sleeping on that stable floor."

"It was a long night, but it had some good parts to it."

The best part shone in Angie's mind, when Horatio had reached out to her and they had lain in the quiet, dark stable, side by side in their warm sleeping bags, holding hands. But she couldn't tell her mom about that. She felt sad, suddenly. Very sad. Even though she loved her mother as much as any daughter could ever love a mom, she realized there were still things that she would never tell her.

She rolled down the window a few inches. "I can feel spring in the air, Mom."

"Oh, I need spring this year," her mother said. "Badly."

"Me too."

By the time they arrived at school, Angie was sing-ing along with her mom:

Home, home on the range
Where the deer and the antelope play...

CHAPTER 14

*O*ver a week had passed since Lila had injured her leg. Horatio hadn't been around once during that time, and Angie couldn't help but wonder if he was avoiding her.

She had wakened early the morning they had slept in the stable and looked shyly over at Horatio. Before that evening they had never touched—not on purpose, anyhow.

When Horatio had wakened, he was all business, rushing to get home in time to change clothes and wash up before school, although there was plenty of time. She had felt self-conscious, but she didn't think she showed it. *He* didn't show anything—just crawled out of his sleeping bag, jammed his feet into his shoes, rolled up his bag and ground cloth, and took off.

Maybe he was angry at himself for holding her hand, giving her reason to think that now he really liked her as a girl, not as the sister of his friend. Maybe he was sorry that he had talked to her about his father, sorry that he had given in to the quiet darkness, the feelings triggered by the three of them sleeping in the stable together. Well, he didn't have to worry! So he had held her hand. The world hadn't changed. The sun still rose in the morning and set at night.

She pushed thoughts of Horatio out of her mind as she approached Lila's stable and heard Owen's deep voice. Owen always sang to a horse as he groomed it. Never the same song twice because he made them up as he went along. Angie loved what she called his homemade songs. Owen called them Owen's blowin's. Now, seeing Owen take the time to help her by grooming Lila, she felt a burst of affection for him. It just bloomed inside her, a big, bright flower. If only she could pick it and give it to him!

"Owen," she said. "Thanks for grooming Lila. She looks happy. She doesn't look like that when I sing."

Owen smiled. He was standing very close to Lila, resting his hand on her back. He had taught Angie that most horses like the feel of bodies close to them. That was why you would see two horses in a pasture standing very close to each other, sometimes with their necks entwined. Often Owen would just lean against a horse as he talked to it.

"How's that wrist of yours, Angie A? Coming along?"

"I guess. But I want it to be perfect right now." She dropped her daypack in the corner. "I can finish grooming Lila now."

Owen handed her the currycomb. "Angie A, Sage is staying at my house for a while."

"Allison told me."

"She's pretty broken up. She won't go to school. She's sure everyone knows about Karl."

"Maybe you should sing to her." Angie knew that was a stupid thing to say, but she felt on guard.

Owen continued as if he hadn't heard her. "The only way I was able to get Sage to come out of the bus was to tell her that I had just bought a horse at an auction that's been badly mishandled. Whoever owned her did a real job on her. She backs into the corner of the stall and won't move when anyone tries to come near. She needs someone who can help her trust people again."

"Did you know the horse was like that when you bought her?"

"I did, but I couldn't sleep at night thinking of her living with that kind of fear. It'll take time and patience to ease her into trusting someone again. I asked Sage to take on the job. That's what got her out of the bus."

"Oh." Angie leaned against Lila. She had seen a horse that had been badly frightened. It had given her terrible dreams. "Does Sage know how to work with a horse like that?"

"She'll have to learn. I'll help her as much as I can."

"Has she started yet?"

Owen nodded. "Two days ago. Sage and the horse seem to have a special affinity for each other. The horse will look at Sage, not at me. So Sage just brings some rope and sits down across the breezeway from the horse and begins oiling the rope and humming, or doing something else that's peaceful for a couple of hours every day. We hope the horse will begin to feel safe enough to raise her head and see what Sage is doing. You know how curious horses are. When Sage feels the time is right, she'll walk close enough to reach out and give the horse the end of the rope. If the horse takes it in her mouth and begins playing with it, Sage will have come a long way. Then she'll work on getting her to accept a halter so she can take her outside."

Angie was listening to Owen so intently that she had stopped grooming Lila. "I'm surprised Sage is patient enough to do all that."

"Well, Sage knows what it is to be mistreated and scared. She seems to relax with the horse. She eats her dinner at the stable now. Soon she'll want to sleep here."

"What's the horse's name?"

"Sage gave her a new name—Starry, short for Starshine."

"Starry—that's a pretty name." Angie hesitated. "Owen, do you think I can see Starry?"

"I wouldn't want you to go alone. Each new person scares her. I can take you now, but just for a few minutes."

"Is Sage with Starry?"

Owen looked at Angie closely. "Why?"

Angie turned away from Owen's gaze. "I just don't want to see Sage, that's all."

"Angie A," Owen said, "I've learned a few things about Sage. Karl isn't her father. He's her uncle, her mother's brother. Sage doesn't know who her father is."

"Karl isn't Sage's father?" Angie shook her head. She felt as if she wanted to run away, not hear any more things she believed were true and now weren't. "Why did he say he was?"

"Maybe he thought it would look better when he was applying for work." Owen paused for a moment. "Maybe Sage liked pretending she had a father. Sage's mother was eighteen when she had Sage. Sage's grandmother raised her. She was ten when her grandmother died. Her mother would take care of her for a while and then disappear. Sage was shuttled back and forth from one relative to another. She had been with Karl for two years. She knew nothing about the check forging. It hit her hard."

Angie took a deep breath. "Everything . . . is so mixed up. I don't know what to think."

"I know, Angie A. It's a lot to take in all at once. I'll check on Starry. If Sage isn't with her, I'll come back for you."

Angie nodded.

Owen left, and Angie turned on the radio, switching channels but not finding anything. She was restless and couldn't concentrate on Lila. She gnawed at a nail without realizing she was doing it until the sliver was between her teeth. How can you stop doing something that you don't know you're doing until you've done it? Maybe she should put bells on each of her fingers, those tiny gold bells people hang on their cat's collar to warn birds away.

Owen finally poked his head in the doorway. "All clear."

Angie had to take long strides to keep up with Owen. When they reached the stable, he paused. "We'll go in slowly. And keep a distance of ten feet. That's the security space Starry needs not to feel threatened."

As they walked toward her stall, Starry, a black and white mare with a white blaze, slammed herself into the corner and stood, head lowered, eyes averted. Her sides quivered.

"Starry," Owen crooned. "Starry, we've come to say hello. Starry, this is my friend, Angie A. She would like to be friends with you. . . ."

The horse didn't move from the corner or raise its eyes.

"Starry, Angie and I are just going to stand here and keep you company for a few minutes. Maybe you'll look at us. That would make us feel good."

They stood, Owen humming. The horse didn't lift its head.

"We're going now, Starry. We'll see you tomorrow. You're a fine horse, Starry and we want to be your friends."

"Oh, Owen," Angie cried when they were outside of the stable. "What could have made her so scared? What did somebody do to her?"

"It doesn't take much to spook a horse. Her owner might have had a bad temper and boxed her in the face when she didn't obey. Or beat her."

"It's so awful. How can anyone do that to a horse?"

"Maybe Sage and Starry can help each other. We'll see."

It was time for the little kids' riding class, so Angie walked to the arena with Owen. She liked teaching the little kids. She hoped it would take her mind off Starry.

"Angie," called Rebecca, a perky eight-year-old. "Help me get on Gentle Sue."

Angie lifted the small girl onto the big horse. But as she walked around the track with Rebecca, all she could think about was Starry, terrified, jammed into a corner. And then her thoughts turned to Sage, hiding in that awful bus.

Owen had said that maybe Starry and Sage could help each other. Angie hoped so.

CHAPTER 15

*H*ere comes Owen," Angie cried, and flew out the kitchen door.

Owen waved as he backed his lumber-filled pickup truck around the circular driveway. It was Sunday and he had set aside time to build Lila's stall by converting the Mordells' storage shed into a stable.

Erik walked out of the house, and his parents followed. They were a regular welcoming committee. Angie was glad. She couldn't pay Owen for the work on the shed by baby-sitting Karama now that Sage was staying at his house. Her dad had wanted to pay Owen, but Owen had refused, and when he insisted, Owen said that maybe her dad could help him draw up a will someday. Angie's mom had already baked two loaves of garlic cheese bread for him to take home. Angie was sure she would add chocolate chip cookies for Karama.

Owen maneuvered his truck through the fence gate and around a tree so that he could park close to the shed.

Erik had asked Horatio to help build the stall and Horatio had said he would. Angie didn't let herself feel excited about that. She couldn't shut off the fact that she was hyper, though. She had no more nails left to bite. It would be the first time she would actually see Horatio since the night in the stable. She had passed him in the hall at school but that didn't count.

Earlier that morning she had hosed the cement floor of the storage shed. Cement was not the greatest surface for a stable but it had the advantage of being completely level. Lila had to be able to stand with her legs in proper alignment if she was to heal properly.

Her mom brought over a thermos of coffee and a half-dozen carrot muffins. She put the tray on an empty barrel.

"Many thanks." Owen breathed in the aroma. "No stable I've been in ever smelled like this!"

Owen suggested that Angie scrape the layers of paint off the window frames so that the windows, stuck now, could be opened. Then he began explaining to Erik the process of building a stall. Angie was scraping away at the paint when she saw Horatio walking through the gate, Silver Chief running alongside him.

"Horatio's brought Silver Chief!" She ran out, calling a greeting to Silver Chief.

The husky responded so enthusiastically that he bowled her over. As she lay on the ground protecting her wrist, he licked her lavishly. She hugged his sturdy body with her good arm.

"I guess he's glad to see you," Horatio said.

Angie wiped her face with the back of her hand. "He's just given me a morning bath!"

Horatio laughed. "I figured Silver Chief could supervise us," he said as they walked to the shed. "She needs exercise. I haven't been able to give her a good run all week."

They were talking. Angie's nervousness, so brittle inside her, melted to milk and honey. It was all right. Horatio had laughed, and looked straight into her eyes. They were over the hump.

Of course, Owen incorporated Horatio into the *men's* work crew, and she continued the piddly *"girl's"* job of scraping paint. But she kept her cool. She felt happy just being in the shed, hearing Owen give directions, smelling fresh bread and newly cut wood, seeing Erik and Horatio work together, watching Silver Chief chase small creatures that raced through the high grass.

"How's the window coming, Angie A?" Owen asked, leaving his work to check on her. "It looks like you're doing a good job."

"Owen . . . I've been wondering how Sage is doing with Starry."

"Sage is doing better with Starry than she's doing with herself."

"What do you mean?"

"She's pretty low. Everyone she's cared about has deserted her." Owen paused. "Sage still hopes that her mother will come and take her home with her."

"Sage has no family that she can go to? No one at all?"

"None of her mother's sisters want her."

Angie was silent.

"Starry is her family now. And she's grown close to Karama."

"I think it's great you've taken her in."

Owen leaned against the wall, his expression thoughtful. "Well . . . we've taken her in, but it'll be a while before she takes us in."

"What do you mean?"

"Sage'll trust a horse sooner than she'll trust a person. Horses haven't hurt her the way people have."

"Owen," Erik called. "This board is warped. I don't think we should use it."

"My boss is calling," Owen said. He laid his hand lightly on Angie's head. "I hope I didn't load your brain with too many heavy thoughts."

At noon, her mom came to tell them that lunch was ready. There was a pot of minestrone soup on the stove and plenty of bread and butter and sliced smoked turkey.

As Angie was walking to the house, Horatio came up alongside her. "Hey, you never told me, did your mom hang the photograph of you and Lila jumping?"

Angie hesitated. "She did, but I took it down."

"Oh."

Angie looked away. "It's hard for me to look at now. Maybe I'll put it back up someday."

"Well . . . maybe I'll take an even better one when Lila's jumping again."

"No, this one is perfect. Really perfect."

As they walked up the stairs to the house, Horatio asked what day that week he could come to muck Lila's stall.

"Oh, you pick it." Angie answered. "Any day except Monday. Erik's going to do it then."

"Wednesday will be good for me. Will it be good for you? But I guess you don't have to be there."

"Oh, I change Lila's bandage on Wednesdays," Angie said. "I'll be there."

CHAPTER 16

*T*hree weeks later on a day Horatio was helping muck Lila's stall, Dr. Rago stopped by to check Lila.

"I thought I'd see how you two were getting along," he said to Angie. "It looks like Lila has good friends."

"This is Horatio, Dr. Rago. He's been helping me. The doctor said my cast may come off next week."

"Good! Let's see if Lila is doing as well as you are. Easy girl," he said as Lila backed away. "I'm not going to hurt you." He deftly unwrapped the bandage.

Angie watched his every move.

"The leg is looking good, Angie. Next time I'll X-ray and we'll get an exact fix on how that bone is doing."

"When would it be safe to move her to our house?" Angie asked eagerly. "Her stable is ready."

"You can take her home in a week."

"In a week! You mean next Wednesday? Horatio, did you hear?"

"Moving a horse to a new stable can be tricky, Angie. Try to be with her as much as you can those first few days."

As Dr. Rago was leaving, Angie asked whether it was all right to feed Lila the cookies she and Beth had baked for her.

"Just don't overdo it. I wouldn't give her more than two a day."

"She loves them. It must be the molasses."

As Dr. Rago walked out of the stall, he paused to look at some poems Angie had taped to the wall. "Lila must be a very literary horse," he said, smiling.

"Oh . . . we had this English project to collect poems on one subject, and I chose horses. I thought I might as well put them up here."

After Dr. Rago left, Horatio looked at the poems. "O.P. probably knows the Shakespeare," he said. He began reading the lines out loud:

" *'I will not change my horse with any that treads.*
When I bestride him I soar, I am a hawk.
He trots the air. The earth sings when he touches it.'

"I bet you know those lines by heart. Let's hear."

"No. You try it," Angie said.

"I remember how it begins. . . ." Horatio looked

straight ahead, as if he were reading the passage on the barn door. " 'I will not change my horse . . . with any that treads. . . .' "

" 'When I bestride him . . .' " Angie prompted.

" 'I soar,' " Horatio said, " 'I am a hawk. . . . He trots the air . . . and sings!' "

Angie laughed. "The horse doesn't sing, the earth does!"

"Well, I knew something sang!" Horatio looked at the poem again. "I came pretty close."

Angie nodded. "Pretty close."

They finished mucking, and when Horatio was ready to leave, Angie asked him if he and O.P. and Evie were coming to their Memorial Day picnic as they had last year.

"Is it a birthday party for you again too?"

Angie blushed. "I don't want it to be. It's my mom's idea."

When Horatio left, making a quick exit, Angie heard him reciting as he ran, " 'I will not change my horse with any that treads. . . . When I bestride him I soar . . .' "

She was sure he was going to try to impress O.P.!

Angie was filling Lila's pail when she saw Sage walk into the stable where Starry was kept. Her short hair was scraggly, and she looked thin.

Angie knew Sage kept to herself at school. She'd see her every once in awhile in the corridor, boots clicking on the tile, eyes ahead, talking to no one.

Angie wondered where she ate. She never saw her in the lunchroom. Owen had said that Sage had been getting good grades before the thing with Karl exploded. Then her grades had crashed. She didn't care about anything anymore, except Starry and Karama. And the dream that her mother would come for her.

Angie found herself haunted by that dream too. She'd imagine Sage up in her room at Owen's, sitting on the bed, crying. There would be a soft knock on the door, and a woman, looking just like Sage, would walk in. She'd put out her arms and Sage would run into them and the woman would rock her like a baby and call her sweetie.

Angie changed Lila's bandage, the second-to-last time she would have to do it, she realized. "Lila," she said, "We should celebrate!" She gave her one of the cookies she and her mom had baked. As she watched Lila devour it, a thought came to her—a shy thought, almost too shy to make itself known. She whispered it to Lila. Lila nudged her face against Angie's cheek.

"Okay, Lila-ba-dila, if you say so." Angie took four of Lila's cookies from the bag in her locker and walked out of the stable. Am I really doing this? she thought, but she kept walking, getting more and more nervous as she drew near Starry's stable. She took a deep breath to quiet her racing heart and looked into the open stable door. Sage was grooming Starry. When she saw Angie, she looked as if she wanted to slam into the rear of the stable the way

Starry had. She said nothing. Just stood there, the currycomb in her hand.

"My mom and I made these special cookies for Lila. I thought Starry might like them, too." Angie quickly put the cookies on a hay bale and left.

As she walked back to Lila's sable, Owen's words echoed in her head. *We took Sage in, but it'll be a long time before she'll take us in.*

Angie guessed you never could know how long a thing like that would take. With horses, or with people.

CHAPTER 17

Angie was watching the minutes crawl by on her watch. At eight thirty she and Smitty would be leading Lila into the horse trailer to drive her to her new home. Angie was so hyper that she had been walking around the ranch for the last half hour talking to anyone who would listen. She didn't want to communicate her nervousness to Lila.

When Allison told her that Smitty's just wouldn't be the same without her and Lila, Angie realized that she had been so intent on getting Lila home that she hadn't thought about all she would miss at the ranch. Smitty's had been her second home for so long. Could it be that she wouldn't see Owen much anymore, that she wouldn't hang out with Allison while they groomed their horses, that she wouldn't have to smile at Smitty's terrible jokes?

Things were never all good or all bad. That fact had become pretty clear to her lately. She was finding out that being grown up enough to own her own horse meant giving up the easy life of being a kid. And if she tried to seesaw back and forth, being a grown-up sometimes and a little kid other times, it didn't work. Not with her dad, anyhow. Now that she was old enough to own her own horse, he expected her to be mature about everything: doing her chores around the house, getting top grades in school, not arguing with Erik. Her mom wasn't that tough on her. If Angie slipped back into being a kid for an hour or even a day, her mom didn't treat her as if she had begun to wet her pants again.

"Owen," she cried as she spotted him walking out of Smitty's office. "Do you remember what's happening today?"

"The Brewers are playing the Yankees."

"Owen!"

Owen grinned.

Angie held up her hand. "And look! My cast is off!"

"Good for you! And Angie A, Sage has good news too. Starry finally took the rope and started playing with it."

"Oh, Owen, that's great!"

"It's the first time I've seen Sage smile in weeks."

"I was wondering, Owen. How long is Sage going to live with you?"

"I don't know, Angie A. So many things are up in the air. Time will tell."

106

"Time will tell," Angie repeated. "That's true of a lot of things, isn't it?"

Owen smiled. "I'm going to miss you, Angie A."

Angie nodded. The lump that rose in her throat made it too hard to answer.

"Let's get rolling," Smitty said. He started talking soothingly as he approached the box stall. "Lila, how are you feeling this morning? Ready for the big move? Angie here isn't. Look at her sleeping in the hay."

"I've been ready for an hour!" Angie said. "I just put Lila's halter on. She seems bothered. Maybe I should have tried to get her used to it a few days ago."

"She'll be all right. Won't you, girl?" Smitty stood quietly by Lila's side for a moment. "Okay, Angie, she's all yours."

Angie hooked on Lila's lead. "Lila-ba-dila, we're going to walk right out of here, and into the trailer for a short ride to your new home. Just come with me. That's the way."

Angie took a few steps, but Lila didn't move. "Come on, Lila-ba-dila. Your leg is all right. Just try and you'll see." She gave the lead a slight tug. Lila took a step forward, hesitated, then took another step, tentatively, as if the ground under her were not quite solid. Angie started humming "Home, home on the range," and slowly led her out of the stable.

Lila hesitated when she reached the ramp leading

into the trailer, but Angie sweet-talked her into moving again, and she slowly walked up.

"You did it, Lila-ba-dila!" Angie said. "Smitty, she did fine, didn't she? She's going to be all right, don't you think? I mean, really all right?"

"Chances are," Smitty said.

If Smitty ever showed any emotion, Angie thought, she'd send up balloons!

It was a gray morning with a faint drizzle in the air. But the weatherman had promised sun, and the breeze was mild. Smitty rode with the window down, and Angie's hair blew in her face. She found a pony-tail holder in her pocket and twisted her hair into it. It was then that she realized she had forgotten her tack box. Oh well, she'd just have to go back later to get it.

Talk about balloons. When they drove up to her house, a bunch of purple ones were flying from the mailbox. "Welcome, Lila," was written in green marker on one of them. Her mom's work. She had had to leave early for a meeting with an editor and felt bad that she wasn't going to be around to greet Lila.

Smitty drove the van through the gate, and by the time they had driven across the field to the stall, Erik had caught up to them. He was breathless from running.

"How'd it go?" he asked as Angie jumped out of the van.

"Fine."

There was no trouble with Lila backing out of the trailer, but at the entry to the stall, she froze. "Lila-ba-dila," Angie coaxed. "You're going to live here now."

Lila refused to budge.

"She's suspicious," Smitty said.

"What do we do?" Angie asked, her heart sinking. Owen had taught her not to push a horse into doing something it wasn't ready to do.

"Lila," she crooned. "Be a good friend and go into your stall. We built it special for you."

Lila put her head down. Her ears flattened, her nostrils flared as she sniffed her new surroundings. She was stone.

"I'll be right back," Smitty said. "I'm going to get some of her old straw from the box stall."

"What'll that do?" Erik asked as Smitty gunned the van and pulled away.

"Lila will smell herself in the old straw and then she might feel safer about going in," Angie said. "I once saw Smitty rub a horse's manure on a saddle so the horse would accept it better."

"Geez!" Erik wagged is head. "Horse people are really nuts!"

Smitty was back in no time at all. He handed Angie two loaded plastic bags. "Spread this old straw on the floor of her stall," he said. "All of it."

Angie dumped the smelly straw out of one bag, raked it over the floor of the stall, then did the same with the other bag. "I notice you're not offering to help," she said to Erik.

"You notice right," he answered. "Geez, that stinks!"

"You're so delicate!" Angie scoffed.

She laid the empty bags outside the stable and stood quietly beside Lila. "Lila-ba-dila. Time to go home."

Lila raised her head and sniffed the air.

Angie took the lead and began to walk into the stall. Lila hesitated, then followed.

Erik started to applaud, and Angie muttered, "Shut up! You want to freak her out?"

"You'd think horses were made of eggshells," he grumbled.

Smitty unloaded two bales of hay on the ground by the door of the stall, climbed swiftly into the van, turned on the ignition and called, "Good luck, Angie." And with that, he was off, across the field, around the driveway, past the flying balloons and out to the road.

"Smitty never gives you a chance to thank him!" Angie said.

"Your wrist is okay now, right, Angie? I don't have to muck anymore?"

Angie frowned at Erik. "You act as if mucking is the absolute worst thing in the world."

He grinned. "You got to admit, Angie. It's a shitty job." He gave Lila a loud kiss on the forehead and was off across the field, his untied laces dangling. Angie could never figure out why he didn't trip and fall on his face.

And now there were just the two of them, she and Lila. Angie looked across the field. How long would it be before Lila would be able to gallop through that high grass? She might never jump, but she *would* gallop. Even if it took working with her for months. Or years.

Then she imagined that the field wasn't empty any longer. A girl on a horse moved swiftly across it. The girl had red hair and the horse was an Arabian with a misty gray mane and tail. Gaining speed the horse leaped effortlessly, her muscled body gleaming in the sun as she sailed over a fence and galloped through the meadow to the woods beyond.

Angie rested her head against Lila's. "Oh, Lila," she said, her voice full of longing.

CHAPTER 18

Angie was in the kitchen eating a bowl of granola. She always ended up with a few oat and bran flakes floating around in a swamp of milk. Her mom was pouring a cup of cinnamon apple tea in an oversize mug. She had taken to drinking great quantities of tea instead of devouring cheddar-cheese popcorn in her ongoing battle not to smoke again.

"Mom, remember, Dr. Rago is coming to X-ray Lila's leg today and I want you to meet him."

"I planned to be home."

"Could we invite him to the Memorial Day picnic? He doesn't have family here. They all live in Iowa."

"It's your birthday party, too. You can invite anyone you like."

"The party's your idea, Mom, not mine! I don't

want all those people singing "Happy Birthday" to me. It's embarrassing."

"You used to love it." Her mother's voice was wistful.

"When I was five years old!" Angie walked to the sink and dumped the leftover milk.

"Angie! I wish you wouldn't waste all that milk. It's a sin!"

"We need a cat to lick it up. Are you sure you haven't outgrown your allergy to cats? Maybe you should get a new test."

Her mom smiled ruefully. "At my age, Angie, you don't outgrow things. You grow them."

At four o'clock Angie's mom left her study and walked to the stable. Dr. Rago had come early and had already taken an X ray.

"I'll call Angie with the results tomorrow," he said. "Lila's looking fine. I think her new home agrees with her."

"It didn't at first!"

"What do you think Lila's chances are for full re- covery, Dr. Rago?" her mom asked.

"I want to study the X ray, but I'm optimistic. Angie's been a wonderful nurse. I'd like to hire her."

"She has been remarkable. I agree."

Angie wriggled. She didn't like being talked about as if she weren't there. But a seed had been planted. Maybe, when she was a little older, she'd be able to work in Dr. Rago's clinic.

Dr. Rago called the next day. Lila's bone had healed satisfactorily. Angie could stop the bandaging and begin taking Lila outdoors.

Such good news! And there was no one at home to share it with. Angie pulled on a sweater and ran to the stable.

"Lila-ba-dila," she exulted, hugging Lila around the neck. "You and I are going to take a walk outside!"

It was a cloudy day, but windless and pleasantly warm. With a sense of enormous significance, Angie put the halter on Lila, then the lead. It had been over two months since Lila had slipped on the ice.

"Come, Lila-ba-dila," she said, gently. "We're going for a very short walk."

Lila hesitated at first, then followed her outside, putting her feet forward tentatively. Out in the field, she lifted her head, inhaled, and then blew the air out in a loud snort.

A good sign! Angie laughed. Lila was enjoying herself. She moved stiffly, but with greater ease as they circled the field. Angie gradually quickened her pace. Lila followed. Then Angie dropped the lead. Lila continued to walk, head erect, ears pointed upward.

"Oh, Lila-ba-dila, you're doing great!" If she hadn't been afraid of freaking Lila out, she would have shouted for joy.

"Oh, Lila! You and I have had a hard time, haven't we? But we're over the worst. Way over!"

Angie walked Lila for exactly ten minutes, then led her back to the stall, hugged her, and gave her a cookie. Lila ate the cookie out of her hand, then let her lips rest in Angie's palm, nuzzling it.

Angie laughed. "Lila-ba-dila, what a wet kiss!"

Instead of going to her room to do her math problems, Angie rode her bike to the ranch. Owen was teaching a class, so she would have to wait to tell him her news. Restless, she began roaming, then stopped when she saw Sage coming out of the stable walking Starry. She drew back in the shadow of a tree and watched Sage and Starry enter the paddock and begin circling it.

Did she dare go closer? She decided to try, and if the signals were negative, she'd back off.

As she approached, Sage's and Starry's backs were to her, but as they rounded the curve, Sage saw her. Her face tensed. She kept walking. Starry's ears flicked forward. She was interested, not fearful.

Angie was suddenly nervous. What do I say? Or do I just keep quiet? Will Sage say anything? Or just act as if I'm not here?

As Sage and Starry came closer, Angie burst out, "Starry looks wonderful. Congratulations."

Sage's amber eyes were wary as she glanced at Angie. "Thanks."

And then Angie was looking at their backs again. Should she wait for them to come around once more, or was this enough for the day? She decided to chance it, and when Sage and Starry approached again, she said quickly. "I started walking Lila today. You can come and see her whenever you want."

Did Sage's face show pleasure? Angie wasn't sure. Sage just said thanks once more and continued circling the paddock.

Angie walked away. Well, she had done it. She couldn't read Sage's body language the way she could read a horse's. She could tell Starry wasn't frightened of her. She couldn't tell that about Sage. People were harder than horses. They hid their feelings. Or shut them off.

She hadn't expected to invite Sage to see Lila. The words had just sprung out of her. Sometimes when words did that, she was sorry. But she wasn't sorry now. The words had seemed right.

As she headed back to the arena to see Owen, she relived the walk with Lila. The knowledge that Lila had actually walked for ten minutes, her gait unhampered, filled her with joy.

Was that why she had been able to ask Sage if she wanted to visit, because she was feeling so good?

What would she be like if she had Sage's life? If she didn't even know who her father was. If her mother didn't want her, just took off and left her to live with relatives who didn't want her either. And now her uncle had dumped her.

Angie thought of the bad moments she had when her mom and dad's plane was late because of a terrible snowstorm. Her stomach had begun to feel like it was being walked on. What if the plane crashed? What if she would never see her parents again?

She stopped and looked back at Starry's barn. The

116

sky behind it was churning with dark clouds that had moved in so quickly, she hadn't had a warning they were coming.

Sage's parents might just as well have been in a plane crash. They had fallen out of her life, and Sage had been horribly hurt. The kind of hurt that could turn you mean, when what you really were was scared. Scared and lonely. She guessed Owen had been trying to tell her that about Sage. But she hadn't wanted to listen—couldn't listen. Then.

Owen was surprised when Angie ran into the arena and greeted him with a shout and a hug. "Owen, the X ray showed Lila's leg is healed. I started walking her today!"

Owen laughed out loud. "Good news, Angie A!"

For a moment Angie thought she would tell Owen that she had invited Sage to visit Lila. But she didn't. Some things were just too private to tell anyone but yourself. And your horse.

CHAPTER 19

Angie had dreamed of this day during the five weeks that she had faithfully hand-walked Lila. Time had moved at a snail's pace. Junior-high graduation was just a few weeks away, and that was both exciting and problematic. Next fall Erik and Horatio would be in high school—still just a year ahead of her, but it would feel like much more.

But at least, as of today, Sunday May 30, she'd be thirteen. A crummy day to be born. Whenever anyone asked her when her birthday was, she'd answer May 30, and they'd say, "Oh, that's Memorial Day." As if that were big news.

Her mom was going to bake one of her spectacular birthday cakes for the Memorial Day picnic. Angie had told her that she didn't want a public cake. Just a private one for the family. This year she hadn't felt like having a party for friends, either. Her party was to be secret and only Lila was invited. But her mom had looked so disappointed that Angie had said, oh, she guessed a big cake would be fine. Double chocolate with raspberry filling.

She woke at six thirty, dressed quickly, grabbed her riding boots, walked barefoot down the stairs and out the kitchen door so as not to wake anyone. When she stepped outside, the porch boards cooled the soles of her feet. Wouldn't it be great to be able to ride in light moccasins the way the Plains Indians had? No boots and no saddle, not all that leather between you and the horse.

Well, she was definitely not a Plains Indian. She pulled on socks and boots and lifted her head as she walked through the field, inhaling deeply, much as horses do when freed from the stable. If she had wanted to let her fancy go, she could imagine the air had been pumped brand new out of that blue bowl of sky just for her. Dew drenched spider-webs suspended between grass blades shimmered in the early morning sunlight. She was careful not to step on a single one with her mighty boots.

As she approached the stable, she was disappointed to see that she hadn't made much progress painting it. Her father had been threatening summer school if she didn't have some useful activities lined up. In desperation she had said that she'd paint the stable, and to convince him of her reliability, she had started on it last weekend. He had insisted on white to match the house. She would have liked barn red.

Lila nickered eagerly as Angie opened the stable door.

"How about a birthday kiss, Lila-ba-dila?" She put her face close to Lila's and Lila nudged her cheek. "Thank you!"

A slip of yellow paper was propped up against the radio. Curious, Angie took it down and read the scribbled words: *I came to see Lila like you said I could. She looks great. Thanx.*

It was signed with a cramped letter *S.*

Over a month had passed since she had blurted out her invitation to Sage. It had probably taken Sage all that time to get up enough courage to come. And then she had to plan it so no one would see her. Angie understood why. She would have done the same thing. It was that security space Owen talked about. Angie folded the note and put it in her pocket.

"Lila," she said. "You're going to give me a ride today." Humming "Home on the Range," as much to relax herself as Lila, she bent and put splint boots on Lila's front legs for support. She laid the plaid blanket over her back, then lifted the saddle off the hook and put it on. No reaction. Then the halter and bridle.

"Oh, Lila," she crooned, "You look so good!"

How would Lila react to weight on her back after

so many weeks of not being saddled? That question had cropped up often during the last week, a weed question that she couldn't pull out of the fertile soil of her mind. She had heard stories about horses who refused to carry a rider once they had been injured and riderless for a long time. But Owen had assured her that those horses had probably been mishandled. She tried to quiet her racing mind.

"Lila, I'm going to mount you, so don't be scared." She led Lila outside. "Now, your leg is fine. And I'm lighter. I've lost three pounds worrying about you."'

She adjusted the reins, placed her foot in the stirrup, passed her right leg over Lila's back, and sank down lightly in the saddle. Placing her right foot in the stirrup, she took the reins in both hands, holding them so they put no more than an even, gentle pressure on Lila's mouth.

Lila seemed unbothered. Angie touched her sides lightly with her boots. "Let's go, Lila-ba-dila."

Lila began to move forward. Angie's mouth was dry, her muscles tight. She had to relax! Lila would feel her tension and become tense herself. She took a deep breath. She wanted Lila to enjoy her first day out.

With each step, Lila seemed to gain confidence and Angie gained confidence along with her. Oh, it felt good to be on a horse again! She breathed in the morning air, feeling the power of the horse under her, the earth under the horse, the blue sky above. She hadn't let herself think about how much she missed riding. Owen had offered her a ride on any horse she wanted, but she had been determined to wait for Lila. And it had been worth it! She wanted to sing out to the whole wonderful world—the birthday present she had dreamed of for so long was hers. She was riding Lila!

Today a walk, in a few days a trot, and then in a week or two Lila might be ready to canter.

Jumping? Well. Time will tell, Angie A.

She was dressing for the picnic when her mom called from downstairs telling her to pick up the phone. Hallie Thompson from Thompson's Stables wanted to talk to her.

As Angie hurried to her mom's study, she recalled that she had last seen Hallie Thompson at a rodeo the Thompsons held in their large arena every fall. They bred horses and Angie liked to ride over to their pasture to see the mares and their foals. There might be as many as twelve foals, each staying close to its mom, pushing its head under her to nurse or sitting under her for shade as if she were a tree. One evening a black filly, still a bit wobbly on her long legs, ventured close to the fence and stared at Angie curiously. Angie reached out and touched the white blaze on her forehead. The filly's mane was short and curly—baby curls Angie called them. She yearned to pick her up, long legs and all, and carry her home.

"Angie," Hallie Thompson said, her voice carrying a hint of her Tennessee drawl. "Vic Rago suggested I call you when I asked him if he knew any high-school girls who might want to spend two hours five mornings a week this summer at the stables with my foals. I try to have my horses spend time with people from day one. Then handling them is a piece of cake. Do you think you'd be interested? Four twenty-five an hour."

"I'm not in high school yet," Angie said, "but I will be next year. And I have my own horse so I'm used to being around them." Her own horse! It thrilled her to be able to say that.

"Well, Vic told me you were a natural with horses. There are specific things I want done: playing with them so they're not head shy, getting them used to having their feet lifted. But I'll show you all that when you come. Mainly, I want them to get a lot of love and attention. Can you start tomorrow?"

"Yes." Was this really happening?

"Kathy Foster's worked for me all year, but she may be leaving town. Is there a girl you might know who could replace her?"

"Oh . . . yes," Angie said, immediately thinking of Allison.

"Well, keep her in mind. I'll know what Kathy is doing by the end of next week. What's your friend's name?"

"Her name is . . ." Angie swallowed hard. "Sage. Sage Sommers."

The Memorial Day picnic began at three, and it was a scorcher of a day. Fortunately, there were benevolent old oaks casting their welcome shade over a large area of the Mordells' back lawn and plenty of room to sit on the assorted chairs, benches, and blankets put out for the event. The long pine table that held a large wooden bowl of fresh fruit would soon groan under the weight of the food placed on it. A net had been set up for those willing to play volleyball under the flush of the sun. For the less active there was croquet near a small grove of crabapple trees. An old hickory held a swing and some climbing ropes.

People began arriving, parking their cars along Bridger Lane. Most of the men wore shorts; many of the women wore sleeveless sundresses. Clothes were balloon bright, echoing the rampant dazzle of yellow, blue, and purple pansies, her mother's pride, that bordered the hundred-year-old farmhouse.

Angie was wearing all white, a risky venture, she knew. But she liked the look of the shirt and shorts she had just bought, and the woven multicolored belt from Guatemala that added color. The Hopi bear pin her parents had given her for her birthday looked great against the white shirt. She had braided her hair, tying it with a turquoise ribbon to echo the turquoise eye of the silver bear.

Erik's birthday present was a piece of amethyst he had seen in a local rock shop. She had been touched.

It was the first present he had given her that he had actually gone out and selected himself. He hadn't wrapped it. Just handed her the amethyst cushioned in cotton. "This is from me," he mumbled, and practically knocked her over handing it to her.

Everyone wished her a happy birthday. She smiled and thanked them and tried her best to be appreciative. Dr. Rago arrived and then Evie, Horatio, and O.P. She greeted them and kept her eye on Horatio, waiting for the moment he was alone to walk over to him. He looked great in jean shorts and a red shirt. Luckily, he hadn't listened to his mom and gotten a haircut.

"Horatio," Angie said. "I have something to show you in the house." She led Horatio to the family room where one wall was completely covered with photographs of family members: grandparents, great-grandparents, her parents when they were married, Angie as a fat baby and as a toothless five-year-old, Erik with his first drum set, her dad sitting behind his desk in his new law office, her mom autographing her latest cookbook.

"You put it up." Horatio stood in front of the photograph he had taken of Angie jumping with Lila. It was in a thin oak frame.

Angie nodded. "Today." She held in her joy just a little. She couldn't quite give it free rein. "This morning I rode Lila for the first time. We went out early for a half hour and she seemed happy." She took a deep breath. "So, I'm not sure if she'll ever be able to jump again—it'll be a while before I can test that—but now that we can ride together, it'll be okay even if she doesn't." She paused, feeling the heat of Horatio's eyes. "So, seeing the photograph feels all right now."

He nodded and looked at the photograph again, this time studying it more attentively.

What was he seeing? Angie wondered. The same thing I am?

He turned back to her. "What a great birthday present Lila gave you."

"The best."

They were leaving the family room when Angie stopped short. "Oh, I have one more thing to show you." She pointed to a photograph of a gray-haired woman. "Aunt Beattie. I finally rescued her from my sock drawer."

Horatio smiled. "She *does* have a long face."

When they walked outdoors again, Dr. Rago and Evie were standing under the grape trellis drinking cans of pop and talking.

"Maybe your mom and Dr. Rago will like each other," Angie said.

Horatio looked alarmed, then shrugged. "He's a neat guy."

Angie's mom rang an old cowbell, calling everyone to eat. Her dad grilled hot dogs, chicken, and hamburgers at the barbecue pit. There were platters of tuna-fish, potato and bean salad, fresh vegetables, cole slaw, raspberry and lime Jell-O molds, and loaves and loaves of her mom's homemade bread and special honey Dijon mustard and garlic butter.

The climax was a spectacular four-layered chocolate cake crowned with white pansies and a circle of fourteen purple candles. Everyone sang "Happy Birthday" and Angie tried to look pleased, but she felt clumsy, as if her arms hung down to her shoes and her smile was rubber. She was much happier passing out slices of the cake, scooping on generous portions of vanilla ice cream for those who liked it à la mode.

"I'm stuffed," Horatio said, sitting down next to her as she settled on a blanket under the crabapple trees.

"Me too. I pigged out on potato salad."

"Erik's back at the table again. I can't believe it."

"My dad says he's got a hollow leg." Angie kicked her sandals off and pushed her feet into the grass. "I got another birthday present today—at least I think of it as a present." She hadn't told anyone but her mom and dad about the job at Thompson's Stables. She wanted to keep it to herself for a little while. She hadn't expected to tell Horatio about it. Sometimes she felt like she had two personalities. One was shy and wanted to keep things private, and the other was talky and wanted to blabber. Horatio seemed to push her blabber button.

"Don't make me guess," Horatio said.

"I've got a summer job. Two hours a day at Thompson's Stables. All I have to do is hang out with the

127

foals, talk to them, hug them, play with them. Mrs. Thompson's one of the best breeders around, and she likes her horses to get used to people from day one. That way the horses grow up trusting people, knowing their smell, the feel of being touched, so they take to being handled like it's a natural part of their life. And she's paying me four twenty-five an hour!"

"Wow. Does she have another opening?"

"She might. But she asked for a girl."

Horatio frowned. "Discrimination."

"I start tomorrow."

"It's like me getting paid to play with some husky pups. Pretty soft!"

"Yeah, I almost feel like I should pay Mrs. Thompson."

She didn't tell him about suggesting Sage for the job. She hadn't told her mother, either. It was one of those things that she told only Lila.

By eight o'clock most people had left to watch the boat regatta at Paddock Lake. Erik went, but Horatio said he didn't feel like it, and would help them clean up. He and Angie folded chairs, put benches back in place, and gathered up garbage bags.

The sun had gone down, and a coolness rose up from the grass.

"Can we say hello to Lila?" Horatio asked when things were back in order.

"Sure."

They crossed the field to the stable under a sky lit

by a luminous moon. The evening air smelled sweet. Lilacs, Angie thought. Her birthday flower.

Lila was glad to see Angie. She nickered and nuzzled Angie's shoulder.

Horatio stroked her ears. "Hi, Lila-ba-dila."

"It's been a long day," Angie said. She gave Lila a carrot she had grabbed from the vegetable platter. "A nice one though. Except for everyone singing to me. I felt so stupid, just standing there. But I loved the cake."

Horatio fidgeted around in his back pocket and, looking embarrassed, pulled an envelope out and handed it to her. "I asked O.P. if he knew a good poem about horses. . . . It's for your birthday."

"Oh . . . thank you." Angie opened the envelope slowly and unfolded a sheet of computer paper. She didn't look at Horatio, afraid of what her face might reveal. She felt so happy, deep down, where happiness didn't always get to.

"I hope you don't have that poem," Horatio said.

Angie shook her head. "I don't." She read to herself:

A Blessing

Just off the highway to Rochester, Minnesota
Twilight bounds softly forth on the grass,
And the eyes of those two Indian ponies
Darken with kindness.

They have come gladly out of the willows
To welcome my friend and me.

We step over the barbed wire into the pasture
Where they have been grazing all day, alone.
They ripple tensely; they can hardly contain their
*   happiness*
That we have come.
They bow shyly as wet swans. They love each
*   other.*
There is no lonliness like theirs.
At home once more,
They begin munching the young tufts of spring in
*   the darkness.*
I would like to hold the slenderer one in my
*   arms*
For she has walked over to me
And nuzzled my left hand.
She is black and white,
Her mane falls wild on her forehead,
And the light breeze moves me to caress her long
*   ear*
That is delicate as the skin over a girl's wrist.
Suddenly I realize
That if I stepped out of my body I would break
Into blossom.

Tears filled Angie's eyes. She wiped them away by rubbing her face against Lila's. "It's the most beautiful poem I've ever read."

Horatio stroked Lila's back as Angie read the poem once more.

"Do you want to walk for a while?" he asked as she

folded the printed sheet carefully and put it in her pocket.

"Sure."

As they moved through the tall grass feathering against their bare legs, he took her hand.